HIDDEN DARKNESS

KEV CARTER

PROLOGUE

No one could hear the noise from the big old farmhouse. It was set back, more than a mile from the main road, with dense woods to the left, arid desolate fields to the right and a lake behind it that was a dark dead stagnant shadow on the local landscape.

No one wanted to visit the place. They had heard about strange things going on up there. Rumours spread and stories were told, each becoming darker and more terrifying as they were eagerly swallowed by the bored residents of the local backwater towns. Tales of the elusive family that lived there became standard teenage folklore. The family was said to consist of at least five members, although there could have been more. Nobody was ever really sure.

The head of the house, without a doubt, was a father, married, to a younger woman, some said they were related by blood, and they had at least three children. Two sons and a young daughter had been seen. It was said that there were more children though this was so far unfounded.

They were a strange lot, never speaking or making eye contact with anyone. When they came into town for food and supplies, they were shunned by the locals without exception. Suspicious mothers grabbed hold of their children protectively until they were out of sight, and people crossed the road to avoid them.

Undeterred by this, even seeming not to notice it at all, they got what they came for from the small but well stocked shops and left without bothering anyone. They had their own generator at the farm, which seemed to run everything. They were quiet, self sufficient and bothered nobody, consequently, they were left to their own devices..

Children would not dare go up to the place because of the stories of witchcraft and the horrifying rumors that the family ate small children. Mothers did nothing to ease their children's fears, in fact they encouraged them. They saw it as a good way to keep them away from the place.

   But there were some who did venture closer, hikers who knew nothing of the family who lived there, run aways and vagrants. Whether they came out or not was another matter. If they did they had never hung around long enough to tell of what they had experienced. —Often screams had been heard be heard from the direction of the farmhouse, The screams echoed through the woods and faded away by the time they reached the town's boundaries. Dogs in the village often disappeared. Many believed it was because of the travelling communities who often passed through, though a handful were convinced that they has wandered a little to far and had found themselves on farmhouse land.

It felt like the family had always been there. Nobody knew where they came from or how long they were planning to stay and nobody was ever going to ask.

It was the pursuit of two convicted criminals that finally altered the course of their existence. For Bob Jackson and Clive Underwood it was the end of the comfortable existence that they complacently accepted as fact.

The helicopter lazily hovered over the area with little interest from the pilot and his mate.

'Can you fucking believe it?' Bob had half an eye on the ground below and they rest on the doorstep cheese and tomato sandwich his wife had broadly prepared at the crack of dawn.

'What you whining about, at least we are in the air and what a day for it'

'It's a day for lazing around the base with the TV on and a couple of cans'

'Something tells me your heart isn't in this job'

'You don't say… Oh fuck.. Jesus H Christ what the fuck!'

The helicopter veered madly to the left as Clive's senses burst into action. Bob might be a lazy bastard but he could spot trouble like no other partner he had ever had and it was the first time he had ever heard him get so agitated.

'Go back, Go back!! Get back there now!'

'Clive's reflexes seemed to be going in slow motion. The helicopter dipped as he struggled to turn it in response to the abject fear in Bob's voice. What the hell had he seen? Surely two cons who had not even managed to use a real gun could not be the reason for Bob's rapidly draining pallor. The adrenal rush kicked in and he expertly maneuvered the helicopter back around to where Bob was pointing hysterically. Bob did not take his eyes of the ground. 'oh fuck..oh fuck.. oh fuck he garbled' manically.

Clive desperately tried to maintain control as he looked down to where Bob was pointing. Sick fear gripped his stomach and he felt the air being vacuumed out of his lungs as he tried to take in what he was seeing.

The man and woman dragged the still body of what looked like a child across the farmyard, each holding a leg, as if they were pulling a sack of rubbish. At first glance the child appeared to be covered in blood. It would not be until they landed that the true terror of what was unfolding would become apparent.

The couple almost appeared to be strolling along, aimlessly chatting as if they were sharing pleasantries. The down draft and roar of the rotor blades made not a damn bit of difference to their task as their steps did not falter. They never even cast a look in the helicopter's direction.

The helicopter was flying really low now, the two men inside on hyper alert as they attempted to absorb what they were seeing.

Bob picked up the mouthpiece for the loud hailer and spoke urgently.

"This is the police. Stand where you are and wait for us to land. Stay away from the helicopter."

Back up officers were already on their way. My God they needed to get here fast.. There was a stunned silence in the cockpit as they waited to see what effect the command had had. Bob felt cold all over. His guts tightened and he felt like he was about to lose his lunch. He

looked in disbelief as the couple carried on ambling along without flinching.

'Jesus Bob, we need to wait for some help here'

'That is a fucking kid down there. Are you suggesting we fucking wait for the bastards to

finish whatever it is they have started? Get down there, we are going to have to sort this

ourselves.'

'Look at them. They are fucking insane. It's like they haven't seen us!'

'We can't just leave them to it for fucks sake, Land the frigging bird!'

'Going against the voice in his head and the hollow feeling in his stomach, Clive dropped the

huge noisy machine into the courtyard of the farmhouse throwing up debris everywhere

They looked at each other fleetingly as Bob heaved his huge frame out of the door.

'Watch my back for fuck's sake'

Before Clive could even reply, Bob sprinted across the courtyard towards the scene. Clive

was paralyzed as his growing sense of unease turned into a tsunami of cold fear,

He watched as Bob approached the unarmed pair shouting to make him self heard over the

sound of the blades. His gut instinct told him it was over before it even began.

As Bob got nearer to the couple, he appeared to make no impact on their stroll and as he got

really close he stared in sick disbelief at the body they were pulling so aimlessly along. The

girl would have been about twelve or thereabouts. Her hair was matted with blood and cold

staring eyes gazed deadly at the sky overhead without expression. The kid was clearly dead.

'Police, Let go of the body and move away' he screamed knowing now that it would not

make a blind bit of difference. Bob knew a lot of things in those few moments. He knew he

should have stayed where he was. He knew he loved his wife and kids and he knew that he

was never going to have the chance to tell them. Without warning the woman dropped the

arm of the dead child and approached him with a blood curdling war cry. Before he had time to respond she kicked him skilfully and violently between the legs.

She then kicked at him repeatedly with her steel toecap boots as he lay on the ground.

She was dressed like a work man and she fought like one, hitting and kicking at the defenseless police officer on the ground, snarling at him as she did. Blood was spilling from his face where her steel boot had smashed into it.

Father watched and did nothing, looking up blankly at the helicopter pilot who was running towards them to try to help his colleague. Calmly and deliberately, Father took something from his side pocket, a long knife which he held up as he stared at the oncoming police pilot. He then started run towards him, screaming at the top of his voice with a shriek like a mad animal and an insane look in his face that stopped the pilot in his tracks.

He turned and ran back to the safety of the helicopter, where he frantically reported the situation and requested help immediately while the father hit the side of the helicopter with his fists and the knife.

It was a terrifying situation and something the pilot had never experienced before, this mad man outside his helicopter foaming at the mouth and insanely slashing the side of the door, snarling and spitting at him.

The sound of police sirens could be heard in the distance, getting closer all the time, but it was already too late for the first officer. He had been kicked so much that his skull had given way and caved in, but he was still being kicked, his head now nothing but a pulp of bone flesh and blood. The floor around him had become a deep crimson pool that was getting bigger.

The pilot could see this and knew there was nothing he could do for his colleague, so he started to activate the controls of his machine to get it airborne again, before the same undoubtedly happened to him.

He brought his machine to life, the giant blades began to turn slowly and the massive engine began revving, ready to power the bird up into the sky. The tremendous downward draft sent all things scattering and blowing in all direction as he slowly lifted the bird up and out of the reach of this mad man, who was looking up snarling and spitting at the hovering machine above him.

The pilot frantically tried to warn the oncoming police officers of the danger they were about to meet, and got an armed response unit on the way also. Fear had gripped him and, although he was out of harm's way, he was still shaking and shouting into his mouth piece for help and back up.

Nothing could have prepared him for this day and it would be one he would never forget. It seemed like an eternity before he saw the cars screeching into the yard from the gate. He was not sure how long it took for them to get there; he was shaking his head slightly not aware he was doing it.

He watched helplessly as the police swarmed out and fought with the two mad persons on the ground; he was in shock and in overdrive, just holding his helicopter up in the air. He was aware of voices in his earpiece, but did not respond because he couldn't understand what they were saying. He slowly moved the helicopter up higher and looked out across the land where he could see more blue flashing lights racing to the scene.

Moving his head slowly down, he looked below and saw the father had been overpowered and was being held down by three police officers, one struggling to put handcuffs on him. Looking the other way, he saw the woman cornered and snarling at the two policemen in front of her, she was shouting at them, grabbing chunks of her own hair and pulling it out as she screamed at them, eventually dropping to her knees, screaming and kicking like a child throwing a tantrum.

The arrival of the ambulance seemed to awake him from his trace-like state and he looked over at his fallen friend as if there was now hope since the ambulance was here, but he knew there was none. A voice echoed in his ears, he shook his head and heard it again.

He was back and he was again in control. He lifted the helicopter high and circled the area, looking from down into the woods and fields on either side of the house, looking over the lake at the back, searching for anyone else who might run from the house. Seeing nothing, he still searched as his commander was telling him to do through the radio earpiece, now completely back to his professional standard and in total control.

He saw the scene unfold below him; saw the cars arriving, saw the armed response enter the house, saw the loud hailers being used, saw the arrests. And he saw his friends body covered with a coat. The sight would never leave him.

It would never leave anyone who was involved. Anyone who saw the sights in the house, anyone who was told of the atrocities of that day and that place and the family who lived there, would be forever affected by it. How could something like this happen in this day and age? Why were the family left alone for so long?

Questions were asked and not answered, people merely wanted to forget and get on with their lives. Some were glad it was over and the horrible family were taken away. Some wanted to go and burn the place to the ground.

It became something of an embarrassment, something no one wanted to talk about. Ignorant and in denial, some town people even refused to admit it ever happened at all, saying it was blown out of proportion and stories were made up. Hiding their own fear and shame, they refused to talk at length about it.

But no one really did know what went on in the farm house, not really, it was all guess work and hearsay. The police found many strange things and made assumptions; experts were brought in, forensic scientists, specialists, and many professionals. But they could only give their opinion, albeit an adept, experienced and practiced one.

The psychiatrists did their best to understand and reach the family. The children were beyond help, the parents were committed insane, the whole incident recorded and logged. No one wanted to know anymore about the family from the old farmhouse, no one wanted to know what became of the children, no one was going to broadcast it anymore, the whole community decided to abandon it and move on.

It was as if they all knew what to do without saying it; no more interviews were given to the press, no television crews were allowed on the surrounding land. The people just played ignorant and said nothing. It would always be there and they had to live with it, as much as they wanted it to go away, it never would. There would always be someone who was curious, someone who wanted to know more.

Eventually it died down, began to be eroded from their memory, or at least put to the back of it, locked away with a psychological key. The place was left, unattended, and derelict; left to rot just like the family who use to live there. No one wanted to live there. The road up to it never used, police came from time to time to check on the place, just in case of vandals, but even they stopped after a while. It was a no-mans land, somewhere no one wanted to visit.

And that is how it stayed for almost two years, left in a time warp, no inhabitants, no visitors; no natural growth of weeds, or plants, just bare earth. The house loomed like some great beast in slumber, holding onto its secrets and its history, waiting until it could come alive again.

And maybe that is how it *should* have stayed, but things never seem to go how they should in these cases. Eventually things began to happen again, life was injected into the old monster and it was about to come alive for a second time, alive with its secrets, and its dreaded past

CHAPTER 1

The train station was old and paint was covering the bad bits of the woodwork, it had obviously seen better times. It was once the most modern and respectable train station around for miles, but somehow it was left behind.

It was not a busy line and therefore didn't make much money, which became apparent when one saw that the old wooden structure of the platform and the waiting room could have been taken right out of a forties film, which was about the time the place was last renovated to any degree.

It was cold, dull and empty looking; the age of steam had passed on, but this platform didn't seem to follow. The most popular visitors were train enthusiasts wanting a bit of history, wanting to see how it was in the day of their beloved steam trains. A bygone age, but not everyone saw it that way, most just didn't like the old, run-down place.

Sitting on a wooden seat waiting for the train to arrive were Ray and his girlfriend of two years, Diane. He was an intense but calm-looking man in early forties, going gray, but in a distinguished way. He was solidly built and sat ramrod straight in his seat, looking down the line.

Diane was seven years his junior and smaller than him by about four inches, making her about five feet seven. She was looking across the platform at a small bird pecking along the line with her hand on her man's knee, resting there as it often does when they are sitting together.

She watched the bird fly away as the track began to rumble slightly. The train blew its whistle and Ray looked at his watch, then at Diane. "Next one's ours."

She nodded and watched as the dirty diesel train pulled into the platform, the smell of it unpleasant to her nose, and the sound ugly; she didn't appreciate trains the way some others did. The train eventually stopped and two sets of doors opened. From the one at the far end,

Ray saw an elderly gentlemen get out and begin to walk towards the exit, minding his own business. To reach the exit he had to walk right past Ray, who noticed that he was in his late sixties and walked in a bit of pain, perhaps arthritis. Ray smiled as he walked past.

The train doors slammed shut and the smelly diesel train pulled away, leaving three young men who had exited from the near set of doors standing on the platform. They were loud and obnoxious, showing off as young men that age felt the need to. One had a can of lager, he drank the last bit and threw the can across the rail line to the opposite platform, much to the amusement of the other two who cheered his action. He held up his hands in triumph and shouted, one would have thought that he'd just scored the winning goal for England in the World Cup with the way the three carried on. Diane took no notice but Ray was watching and he tensed up slightly. Feeling it, she took his hand and held it.

The old man was walking towards the three and tried to get past them as quickly as possible, but they waited for him and the loudest stood in front of the other two, who were watching him. Without warning, the first one punched the old man hard in the face, dropping him to the floor in pain and fear. All three cheered again, acting as if they had done some great deed.

"Please," pleaded the old man from the floor, his mouth was bleeding from the punch and he had fallen awkwardly, hurting himself further.

"Shut up, you stupid old fucker," the young man said as they all laughed at the sight of their victory over an old man in his sixties.

At this Ray stood and walked over to them. Diane tried to hold him back, but couldn't stop him. He calmly walked up to the first man and hit him hard right in the face, throwing him backwards onto the floor.

"Hurts, doesn't it?" he asked, then, looking at the other two, he stood waiting to see what they were going to do. They looked at their friend on the floor, holding his bleeding face.

Diane came over and helped the old man up. Steadying him, she walked him to a seat and sat with him, where she took a hanky from her trouser pocket, dabbing his mouth for him.

Ray stared at the two men standing in front of him. They were unsure what to do and looked at each other questioningly. It was obvious to them that Ray was solidly built, and they found his confidence a little unnerving.

"Think you're funny, do you? Hitting old men" he said, not taking his eyes off of them. Not even when the first man began to rise from the ground.

Ray hit him twice with a left hook, much harder than his first punch. The man went down with a hard thud. When his friends saw that he wasn't moving, they became nervous, swallowing hard and backing away slowly.

"Why do you little bastards do this sort of thing?"

"Sorry, mate," one said unconvincingly.

"Yeah, sorry, we didn't know you knew him," the other one said.

"I don't need to know him."

"Leave it, Ray, please," Diane shouted.

"What I want to do is smash the shit out of you, but I don't have the time right now, so pick your fucking tosspot of a friend up and piss off. And if I ever see any of you again, you won't walk away, do you understand?" His voice was calm but they knew he meant what he said.

They both took their unconscious friend and left without saying a word or even looking back. One took his legs, the other took his arms, and they left the platform carrying their friend. Ray stood and watched them. If he was not so angry, he would have thought the sight was comical.

Turning back to Diane and the old man, he came over and smiled down at the shaking gentleman. "You alright, mate?"

"Yes, thank you," he said, still shaking and holding the hanky up to his lip.

Ray looked to where the three men had gone and shook his head, then looked back down at the man, asking, "Is there anything we can get you, friend?"

"No. I'm very grateful to you for your help. I don't know what I did wrong to those men."

"You didn't do anything wrong, my friend, nothing at all. The world is full of wankers like that. Ray knelt on one knee, looking him in the eye. "Are you sure you're okay?"

His blood boiled at the pathetic sight of this helpless man who, for no reason, was punched and God knows what else if he had not been there. He felt like going after them, although, even as he stood and looked in their direction, he knew he should let it go.

"Is someone coming to meet you?" Diane asked the gentlemen, glancing up at Ray as she did.

"No, I am going to get a taxi home. Thank you so much, you are very kind," he said as he stood and steadied himself, handing the hanky back to Diane who gestured for him to keep it. Ray walked with him, and Diane watched as they went out of sight, sighing and returning to the bench they had been sitting on originally.

It was not long before Ray was walking back after seeing the man safely into a taxi. He walked up and sat next to her without looking at her. He sighed and said, "Go on then."

"Well, for fuck sake, I know it was not right but I have my two kids coming on the next train. What if it had turned nasty?" She was annoyed; he could hear it in her voice and see it in her body language as she sat with her arms folded tight and her legs crossed, looking down the line.

"It didn't and they deserved to be fucking smashed, if you ask me. It makes me sick to think that this is the world we live in, an old man gets smashed in the fucking face for no reason and the wankers that do it think it's funny. What a lovely place this is. I'm sorry, but I can't just sit here and let it happen. If I had time I would have--"

He wasn't able to finish before Diane told him, "Yes, yes, I know. I don't agree with it either, but for God's sake, Ray, my kids are coming and the last thing I want them to see is you brawling with three men on a fucking station platform. What would I have done if they had got the better of you? Where would that of left us?"

He slowly turned and looked at her, "They didn't and I knew they wouldn't. They're all the fucking same, that kind, one mouthy one and the others follow. Smash down the hard one and the others don't know what the fuck to do. Anyway, it gave me some satisfaction. That poor bloke did nothing wrong. I should have crippled the fuckers."

"Yeah." She looked away for a moment before taking his hand in hers and squeezing it. He returned the squeeze and she looked at him and smiled.

"Sorry," he said, without expression.

"It's okay. He went down like a sack of spuds, didn't he?" She smiled and a little laugh came from her lips.

"I didn't hit him hard the first time because I wanted to hit him again."

"Fucking wankers!"

"Exactly."

"Where did they go?"

"Don't know, I didn't see them after they went off around the corner. I saw the old chap into a taxi and came back." He shook his head and squeezed her hand. "What a shit world we live in, Babe," he sighed, looking down the line.

"Yeah, but don't tell anybody because no one wants to know."

The train was not to long in coming and again Diane pulled a face at the noise and smell of the thing. But her frown changed into a smile when she saw her two children get off the train. They had been visiting their dad and were coming to stay with her and Ray for the holidays. She was excited about seeing them and their little faces lit up when they got off the train and saw their mum.

Amber was ten years old, small and thin, although she had begun to put weight on lately. She was cheeky looking and wore round rimmed glasses, which she often pushed up with one finger.

Behind her was Tommy. He was twelve though he looked older and he was conscious about the spots that had been breaking out on his face and neck; acne was making itself obvious, much to the amusement of his mischievous little sister, and he hated it. He had a mature head on his shoulders and the voice that was once high-pitched had begun to change, becoming much deeper and much more mature. He walked close to his sister, looking after her; she was not always nice to him, but he was loyal and would not let any harm come to her.

Amber pushed her glasses up with her finger and pulled her jeans up from one side where they always seemed to drop, running to her mum and throwing her arms around her with loving look on her face.

"Hi, Baby," her mum said, returning the hug.

"Hi, Mum, love you," she replied, kissing her.

Tommy came walking up and nodded to Ray. "Alright, mate" he said like an old friend.

"How are you doing?" Ray asked and held his fist up while Tommy did the same and they touched knuckles. Amber came over and hugged Ray and kissed him as Tommy hugged his mother and told her he had missed her.

The train pulled away and they were all left on the platform, Ray made the move to leave and they all followed.

"Did you have a good time at your Dad's?" Diane asked them as they walked.

"No," was Ambers answer, short and sweet.

"It was alright." Tommy commented without any enthusiasm, walking faster to catch up to Ray, leaving the two ladies were chattering away.

"So, what is this place like then, mate?" Tommy asked.

"Old and needs a lot of work, but it's very private and secluded, so no one will hear you scream." He looked down and smiled a mock-evil smile.

"Oh, yeah?" Tommy kept pace with Ray, matching his stride and lifting himself up taller as he did, walking alongside him as much his equal as he could, or thought he could.

Where his dad was strict and always finding fault, Ray seemed much more as ease and let him get away with much more. Tommy swore when he was with Ray, when his mum wasn't about, that is, and that would be something his dad would not let him get away with. He liked Ray, but it was not always the case; when his mum first met him and they were all getting to know each other, he didn't like him at all, but now he thought Ray was ok.

Amber had always liked Ray, but then again, she likes most people.

In the beginning, it was hard for Diane to work out how to introduce them and bring them all together as a family. She knew Ray would never try to take their father's place and she told them that. However her biggest concern was that Ray had no children of his own and she wondered if he could adjust to a life with them. Until now, they had lived their own houses, but here they were all going to be together, just like a real family. It was something she had wanted for a long time and she was very happy it was now becoming a reality.

They all got into the old Ford Sierra with Ray proudly driving. He loved this car and had practically rebuilt it entirely over the years he had owned it. The blue car was becoming a classic and had never let him down.

They all put their seat belts on and, when they were ready, he started the two litre injection engine and smiled with a proud grin as she roared into life on the first turn of the key. Letting off the hand brake, he eased out of the car park.

"You need a newer car, Ray, this one does nothing for my street cred at all," Tommy said, looking around with a grimace at the old cloth seats and interior.

"I was driving this car before you were born, son. It's a bloody classic."

"Yeah, but it's old and falling to bits. Isn't it about time you traded this in?"

"It's not what you're given, it is what you do with what you have got."

"You need a new car, Ray" Amber says, while looking out of the window.

Diane looked over at him from the passenger's seat and smiled. "It sounds as if you're outnumbered."

"Well, all of you could walk," Ray stated while pulling out of a junction.

"Probably get there faster," Tommy said, smiling at his mum who had glanced back at him. Amber giggled and put her hand up to her mouth, then pushed her glasses up with the same hand.

Ray pressed on the accelerator and the engine roared as the car sped up with effortless grace. "This car, my friend, always has more than enough power, it even accelerates up hills."

"How old is it, about fifty years?"

"Sod off, you little shit. When you can drive and can afford a car, you can have an opinion. Until then shut up"

"Ooh," the three say in unison, mocking him jokingly. They all laughed and Diane looked at Ray with a smile, patting him on the knee. When he looked at her, she winked at him. "Cheeky buggers, none of you have any idea what this car is or means to me. It is part of me, my past, a better time. Cars are not built like this any more. Do you know what I had before this? A Cortina."

"A what?" Tommy asked.

"Exactly, you have no bloody idea."

"I'm modern, I don't live in the past" Tommy stated.

"Well I wouldn't brag about that too much if I were you, modern is shite."

"No it's not, it's better than the old stuff."

"Bollocks, old is good, old is better."

"You're only saying that because you're old" Amber remarked, still looking out of the window. Tommy laughed, and so did Diane.

"What is this, 'pick on Ray' day or what?"

"It's a lovely old car, Babe" Diane told him, patting the dash board.

"None of you have any bloody idea, you bunch of ignorant know-nothings."

"*Young,* ignorant know- nothings," Diane added.

"You're not that far behind me, my dear, and with old age comes experience."

"And gray hair," she said with a smile. Hearing the children giggle in the back of the car, she looked back at them, winking in a joking manner.

"Old is good, better than modern rubbish" Ray said.

"If you say so, dear." Diane looked out of the window and watched the world speed by, thinking about how happy she was with Ray. He is all that she ever wanted, and now that they are going to live together, she was very excited. She had never met anyone like him before and she loved him the very first time she saw him. Over time that love had grown and she had grown with it; she found that spending time with him made her feel complete. After her children, he was the most precious thing in her life and nothing would ever take her away from him.

She glanced at him as he drove, his handsome face looking intense and so sexy, and she smiled to herself. Never could she remember feeling so happy, nor could she imagine life without him. Sometimes she found herself crying, she was so happy with her man. She told

him she loved him every day; her dad told her from the time she was a small girl that if you

find someone you love, tell them every day and never let them go, and this is what she

intended to do.

He was hers and no on one else would ever get near. She didn't want anyone else, and

she made sure he didn't want or need anyone else either. They were going to grow old

together and have a long happy life with each other. She found herself smiling at the thought

and it made her feel content and secure. What more could she ask for?

CHAPTER 2

The estate agent had been waiting for nearly ten minutes already and was becoming impatient. Not that he had anywhere else to go, he just didn't want to be here, waiting outside this place. He pulled his tie down a bit and wound the car window down to take a deep breath of air. As he glanced over at the farm house, a shiver came over him, so he wound the window back up.

"What's wrong with you?" his colleague asked.

"I don't want to be here, I just want to give them the keys and be gone." He had a nervous quiver to his voice, much to the amusement of his colleague who smiled and shook his head.

He was a younger man, new with the firm, and he was enjoying the job so far. He turned to face other man in the car and saw that he was genuinely nervous. "What are you so bloody scared about?"

"If you knew what happened here, you would be scared too." He looked at him and swallowed, wiping a bead of sweat from his forehead.

"Oh come on, I know the stories. They get scarier every time they're told."

"Listen, my cousin is in the police and he was one of the poor bastards who had to go in there and find that stuff. Fucking hell, they should of burnt this place down, not sold it at auction. And I'll bet no one has told the poor fuckers that bought the place."

"Surely they know the stories, it was all over the papers and news."

"They're not from around here, are they? No one around here would buy the place. She is a teacher, she's got a job at the school, and they're coming here to do the place up during the summer holidays before she starts her new job. They have two kids who start the school as well and I'm not sure what he does."

"You've never met them?"

"No, just talked to them on the phone. They bought it at auction and have never even seen the bloody place. Bloody stupid, buying this house. Who knows what's still in there"

"You're a right salesman, you, I must say."

"This house is evil, lived in by demented, evil people. You mark my words, something horrible will happen there."

"Just because the people were bad doesn't make the house bad."

"You don't know what they did, what they worshiped, how many people went in and never come out. They killed bloody dogs, used to get them and kill them, fucking dozens of the things."

"Dogs? Why dogs?"

"I don't know, they were evil. They killed their own children, tied their daughter down and sliced her up like a pig, he used to fuck his wife with the butt end of a bowie knife then cut her with it, it turned him on. He cut her until she bled, then rammed the butt end of the knife up her pussy, sick fucker"

"You don't believe all that shite, do you?"

"My cousin told me stuff you wouldn't believe. They worshiped the devil in there, had Ouija boards and tried to contact the dead. They killed and ate tramps, travellers, God knows who else, anyone unlucky enough to stray in there, I guess."

"Now you are just being silly."

"Silly? Fucking hell you weren't here when it was happening, it makes me shiver just thinking about it." He shivered in his seat and shook his head.

"So, where are they now?"

"Locked up in a nut house. They found two children in there, and the one they killed, but some people say there is still some left living in the house and on the grounds."

"Still living in there?" He looked out of the window and up the drive to the old house, he didn't know what he was looking for, he just felt compelled to look.

"I wouldn't go in there for a million quid, no fucking way, they should--"

"Burn the place down, I know," he finished his sentence for him, still looking up at the place. He opened the door and got out.

"What the hell are you doing?"

"Going to have a look about." He stood and straightened his jacket.

"Get back in the bloody car now!" his colleague shouted at him.

"I'm not afraid of all that gossip and rubbish"

"Get in this fucking car," his voice was serious and intense, it shocked his colleague for a moment, but as he looked down at him, he slowly got back into the car, saying nothing more; he just sat there, confused, and curious.

"Right listen to me, I don't give a shit what you think, or how brave you think you are. I know what happened and I know stories from my cousin that never were put in the papers, so when I tell you your going nowhere near the place, you're not, is that clear?

"You're new around here son, I was born here. I know what you think and I don't give a fucking toss, you can call me stupid old fucker, silly twat, superstitious git, what ever you want. Something is very wrong with this place and neither you or me are going to say a bloody thing to these people. They have bought it and it's up to them to live with it, we're just glad to be shut of it, is that clear?" He put his face close to his colleague's, staring him right in the eye.

"Yes, but surely they should have been told."

"It's up to them, they have bought the bloody place and every thing that comes with it. If I told them what went on there, they wouldn't believe me, just like you. If I said dead bodies were found in there, cut up, half-eaten and there might be bodies still buried in there, what would they say?

"The police did a search, but my cousin said they didn't have the money and the search was nowhere near as intense as it should have been. They have killed more then they have found, you mark my words."

"I think they should be told, Dave."

"No one says anything; they have bought the place and the history that comes with it. Fucking hell, they got it so cheap they should have known something was wrong. No one round here for miles wanted the place; it's cursed and no one will get me in there."

"What if they want showing round?"

"Why the hell do you think you're here," he said, turning and looking at him coldly.

"Me?" He swallowed hard, his bravado of a few minutes ago had gone and nervousness had taken its place.

"You just be bloody careful and get in and out as fast as you can. Just give them the keys and go, try not to go into that place. Say you have an important meeting or something and you can't stay."

"Fucking hell!"

"Yeah, well, welcome to the job, my friend. Don't worry, you will never get anything like this again. This house is a bloody omega and should be burnt to the ground."

"What is it like inside?"

"Cold and dead, just like the people who lived in it."

"I thought they were in a nut house?"

"Just give them the keys and get away. Why the hell they had to make it after office hours I don't know."

"What about electricity and gas and stuff?"

"We don't want to be here long, so don't linger, okay?" He looked around with a nervous look on his face, glancing for a moment at the house then looking away again quickly.

"Is there any electricity?"

"Yes, it all works. With any luck it will short and cause a fire and the place burn to the ground."

"You're beginning to sound like a broken record. You really don't like this place, do you?"

"No. It is evil and no one in there right mind should live in there."

"Well, someone's going to."

"Fucking idiots." He looked at his watch and then at the clock on the dash to confirm the time, he slumped back into his seat with his arms folded, restless. Every now and again he glanced up at the house then away again. His nervousness showed and he didn't care, he just wanted to be away from this place.

"Tell you what, I'll bet it is a desolate place at night, creepy and cold. Does it have heating?"

"Don't know, don't care. Where the bloody hell are they," he looked at his watch again and out through the back window of his car.

"Bet it is a right mess in there, what if they want showing round?"

"Then show them round, big man. Let's see how brave you are."

"I wish they would hurry up, what time were they suppose to be here?"

"Ten minutes ago, he said looking at his watch again, I will give it another five minutes then I'm going, sod it"

"We can't do that, can we?"

"I'm here on time, it is their fault if they miss us, they should have been punctual shouldn't they," he said as he looked at his colleague and started the car.

"What are you doing?"

"I'm going. You can stay if you want." Just as he says this a car comes into sight slowly coming up the hill, a Sierra with a man and woman in it as well as some kids in the back seat.

"Is this them?" he nods towards the approaching car.

"Fucking hell." Dave turned off the engine and everything was quiet again.

"Here they are," his colleague watched as the car pulled through the two old wrought iron gates and up the spacious drive leading to the front entrance of the house.

"Ok, right, give them the key, say we are in a hurry and we've got to go. You got the keys?" Dave pushed him out of the car before he could answer. Gathering himself, he stood, gently closing the door behind him. He slowly walked up to Ray, who was already out of the car watching him, while the woman leaned over the back seat talking to the two children.

He felt a nervous shiver run down his spine and contemplated telling them to get back in their car and leave, but he knew he wouldn't. He forced a smile as he reached Ray, he holding out his hand. "Hello" he said, as they shook hands.

"Alright, mate" Ray said in his usual manner.

Diane got out of the car and smiled as she walked up to him, holding out her hand. He shook her hand as she gave him a friendly nod. "Sorry we're a little late. We hope it's not thrown you out any."

"No, but we have another appointment to go to," he said as he held out the keys.

Before he could say anything else, Ray told him, "Ok, you get off then and we will take it from here." He took the keys and smiled.

"Oh, right, thank you. If there is anything you need to know, don't hesitate to get in touch with our office. I hope you are okay here and that it is everything you wanted." He was relived and it showed in his voice. Before anything else could be said, the car was started and the two men were gone.

Ray stood and watched them go while Diane shook her head in disbelief. "Well, the ignorant bastards."

"Sod em, it is much more adventurous to explore the place ourselves anyway. He's probably never been in the place and knows nothing about it anyway."

She stood next to him and they both looked at the old place. The children were looking out of the car window, and it was obvious that they were not impressed. Ray, though, was smiling and looked very satisfied. Diane, holding his hand was just happy that he was happy. She looked round the grounds, noticing that the courtyard was sizable, much bigger than she remembered from the photos they had seen.

"It is older than I imagined, and more run down."

"It has character and it's old, so it's built to last. We knew there was a lot of work to do. And we have no bloody neighbours to bother us." Ray told her as he looked up inspecting the gray slate roof.

"Oh yeah, I'm not complaining." She pulled him closer and he put his arm round her.

"Gray slate roof," he said, nodding up to it.

"Is that good?" she asked.

"Best roof you can have, it will last until the house falls down. My dad used to put these on, and used to turn em as well."

"Turn them?"

"Yeah every few hundred years you just turn the slate over and it looks like new."

"Oh, that's clever," she said. She looked back at her children still in the car and she let go of Ray to open the doors and let them out while he walked closer to the main building. They both looked at her incredulously. "Mum it's a derelict house." Tommy said, looking unimpressed at the old building in front of them.

"It looks like it is going to fall down," Amber remarked.

"Stop being silly. Remember what we said, it is going to be a bit difficult to begin with, but we all have to pull together and help each other. This place will be a great and you will both come to love it here, I promise."

The children looked at each other unconvinced. Seeing Ray standing near the front door, they followed their mother to him. He turned and smiled at Diane as she came up, but stopped smiling when he looked down at the children. "What is the matter with you two?" he asked firmly.

"Nothing," they both reply, looking at each other.

"Listen, you will come to learn just what a fantastic investment this place is. It has a stable over the back, Amber, just right for a pony in the future. She smiled at the idea and looked at her mum, who nodded. "Tommy, I would have died for a chance like this when I was your age. You don't know the fun you can have here, son."

"Well, I will try Ray. It's just not what I expected. It's a bit old and run down." He looked around and the unhappiness on his face was apparent.

"Listen Tommy, you are going to have to dig in and work like the rest of us. We never said it would be easy but the rewards are going to be amazing, you will see," Diane told him.

"Can I really have a pony, Ray?" Amber asked, smiling widely.

"Eventually. It will take some time, but eventually."

"Oh yeah, what a great place this is!" she said excitedly.

"Oh yeah, bloody great place," Tommy said under his breath looking round the yard.

"Right then, shall we go in?" Ray asked as he put the key in the lock and turned it. It opened with a click and he pushed the door open, the hinges were a little stiff but he managed it with ease. The place was dark, but the light from outside flooded the hallway, as if the place had just come alive.

CHAPTER 3

He stepped in and the joy on his face was obvious. He smiled as looked around, seeing an investment and a chance to build a life in a house as he had always wanted, a chance to renovate, to rebuild, to decorate, to furnish.

What Tommy saw was an dusty old place with ancient-looking items in it, no light modern décor, nothing at all of interest to him and he instantly hated the place. Everyone was standing together in the entry, each seeing something different, and most of what they saw wasn't to everyone's liking.

Walking into the main front room, Ray went to the curtains and opened them, letting light fill the room. He looked around now sunny room, which made it look even more derelict. The moist smell in the air and the damp feel just gave the house character in Ray's eyes, it just made it uncomfortable and horrid to Tommy.

Diane was the first to speak, in an attempt to lighten the mood and get their adventure off to a good start. "Well yes, it is old and it is dirty, but it is ours, and with a lot of work it will be magnificent. Just think, kids, you will both have your own room, you have not had that before. And they're big rooms as well, double rooms, how great will that be?" She smiled down at the two children, trying to encourage their enthusiasm.

"Yes and I will have a pony" Amber smiled with a gleaming smile that melted her mother's heart.

"Lovely, and what do I get?" Tommy said to no one in particular.

Ray looked at him with a disgusted glare and Amber said nothing. It was left to Diane to try and right things again. "You get a future, son. Stop being so bloody ungrateful and start brightening your attitude, lad. We told you it was going to take some work, look at it as an adventure, not a bloody misery"

"But it's old, Mum, where have you brought us?"

"Come on, lets go and look at your bedroom," she said, leading her children up the stairs. Ray, stood in the room and shook his head with a sigh, then he walked into the back room, which was not as large as the front. To the left of this was the kitchen. The place had been emptied and was bare inside, nothing left but dirt and dust. Fortunately, they both had enough furniture and appliances to fill the house.

He could hear footsteps upstairs on the old wooden floorboards as Diane showed the children their new rooms. Looking out the back window he watched a bird land on the small fence around the garden, which had been dug over at some time but was now left bare except for a few weeds. The small bird took flight again, up and across the field.

He noticed a trail which led into a small patch of woods and he was looking forward to walking his faithful dog there. He sighed again, this time with contentment; he was very satisfied with the place and was so pleased he had bought it.

Walking back into the hall, he climbed the wooden stairs, which creaked under his weight, and he noticed that the banister was slightly loose as he pulled on it. When he reached the top landing, he could hear Diane's voice once again telling her son to appreciate his new home. He was again moaning about the 'oldness' of it, as he put it.

Amber, however, was happy to roam around the place. She smiled at Ray and pointed to a front room, saying as she passed, "That is going to be my room, Ray," then she was gone again, exploring another room to the back. He watched her disappear into it then walked slowly in to Diane who was on one knee in front of her son, looking at him with pleading eyes and holding his hands in hers saying,

"Look son, we are here and that is the end of it, there is no turning back. You are starting a new school soon and you will make new friends, just think of the fun you can have round here with your mates in the future. We will be getting all your stuff over soon and then you can start to think about decorating your room." Her words were landing on deaf ears; he was not interested, he didn't like it and that was the end of it in his mind.

"You should think your self lucky, lad," Ray told him from the doorway.

"Lucky? How can I be lucky living here?" The boy's attitude infuriated Ray and he was about to explode, but Diane held up her hand and stopped him.

Turning to Tommy, she took him by the shoulders, "Now you listen to me, I am not having this attitude. You are here to stay. This is now your home. Ray and I have put all we have into this place and you'd better just stop being so bloody selfish or I will tan your arse, do you understand?" She was shouting at him and when she did this, he knew she meant business.

He nodded and looked to the floor. "Sorry, Mum" he said quietly.

"And what about Ray?"

"Sorry, Ray" he said with out turning to look at him.

"You should wise up, lad. I would have given my right arm to live in a place like this when I was your age. We didn't have bloody computers and game consoles then, we made mates and spent time outside, exploring and having adventures. There is more to life than sitting in front of a fucking computer screen."

Annoyed, he walked away, hearing Diane talking to her son again as he went. He walked into one of the back bedrooms and looked out over the fields at the back of his new home, then he heard Amber walking past the room and heading off into yet another one down the hall. This is what he had expected Tommy to do instead of just sulking.

As he stared out the window, lost in thought, he was aware of someone coming in behind him. Turning, he saw it was Diane.

She smiled and stood next to him, they both looked out of the window as they spoke. "Nice view," she said.

"Bloody lovely. It's a great place."

"Yes it is. Just try not to get angry with Tommy, it is hard for him to adjust to all this, you know. He will come around."

"He needs to harden up a bit. Little Amber is off exploring--fucking hell, I would have been all over the sodding place at his age," he said, shaking his head.

"Yeah, well he will be, eventually, he just needs some time to bed in. Please don't be mad at him." She turned to face him, but he continued to look out of the window.

"It's not the end of the world because he can't play a silly game on a computer. He should be out there, fighting, climbing trees, making mates, falling over, getting cuts and bruises. Fucking hell, you are only young once."

"Ray, look, I know they are not your kids, but we talked about this didn't we? You are going to have to adjust as well, it works both ways. You have never lived full-time with children before, so you are on a learning curve also. You are going to have to learn together. I'm not going to be the pig in the middle all the time."

"He wants to harden up, the bloody jam puff." He turned to face her and took her in his arms; she snuggled up to him, feeling warm and safe.

"He is not a puff," she said into his chest.

"Makes me wonder. When I was his age I was always out, getting into scrapes and fights, it is part of growing up. That is what's wrong with the kids of today, they spend too much time indoors, looking at silly games and computers."

"Well, times change, love."

"For the worst if you ask me. Fucking hell, I would have got a rope by now and had a swing up in one of those trees over there." He looked out across the field to the small wood in the distance, thinking to himself for a moment what a time he would have had as a child there.

"Just give him a bit of space, not every child is a rogue like you were," she said, smiling and playfully pinching his ribs.

"Fight or flight where I grew up. It did me no harm, makes you stick up for yourself. What would Tommy do if someone came at him looking for trouble, challenge him to a game on his computer?"

"Well, you will have to teach him, won't you?"

"His dad should have done all that."

"His dad has never had a fight in his life"

"I still think he needs to harden up a bit." He pushed her away from him, holding her at arms length, "This is going to be a great adventure, babe, and we will make this place our palace. This is what I have always wanted."

"I know it is, I feel the same. And so long as we're together, I will have a perfect life" she kissed him and they then walk out of the room arm in arm.

When they arrive at the landing, they find Amber. "Well, when you two love birds have finished, is it okay if I go outside to see where my pony will be staying?"

"You're not having one yet. It will be a while before we get round to that, darling, we have the house to fix first," her mother told her with a smile.

"Oh, I know, but I like to be prepared. I won't go far." She headed off down the stairs and was gone in a few moments, heading outside. Ray found himself smiling at her, then he looks up towards Tommy's room. Finally he looked down at Diane, who was looking up at him with loving eyes.

"A little time?" he asked.

"Yeah, just a little space, eh?" she nodded at him with a wink.

"I don't know what this world is coming to."

"Well I don't care," she said, wrapping her arm around his waist. "I have all I want right here; my kids, my new beautiful home and my handsome man. What else could I ask for?"

"We will make this place work, babe, it will be bloody fantastic this time next year. It will be a lot of hard work, but it will be worth it in the end. You only get out what you put in," he said, nodding.

"I can't believe how lucky we were to get it so cheap," she said as she looked around the room, nodding in satisfaction.

"Come on, let's have a look around then," Ray said, taking her hand and leading her out of the room to explore the rest of the house.

Outside, Amber had roamed off to one side of the courtyard where she had found two barns, one much larger than the other. The large one was empty and dull-looking, run-down and dirty, she didn't go any closer to this one because, for some reason that she couldn't explain, it made her a little nervous.

The smaller one was much nicer and she stood just inside the opening where there should have been two doors here, but they were now missing. She looked in and could see it needed cleaning and clearing out; there were old bits of machinery and an old, rusty bike at the back, as well as some grass growing from the wall and a leaky roof that she could see sunlight shining through.

She put her hands on her hips and, as she looked around, said to herself, "Ray, you have a lot of work to do in here before I can keep my pony happy and safe."

As she walked further in, she noticed there was a ladder at the far end which was leaning on the edge of a platform leading up to a elevated part of the building. From her spot on the floor she could not see what was up there, so she walked to the bottom of the ladder and decided that it looked very far up, besides being too dark.

She turned and walked back towards the front, passing through patches of sunlight as she did. Although she could not see up the ladder, what was up there could see down and the red, bloodshot eyes watched her every move in silence.

Skipping out of the place, she headed back to the house. She looked up and saw her mother looking out of the upstairs window, they waved at each other and she then headed off to the rear of the house.

"Well, Amber seems to like it," Diane said to Ray, turning back to face him, but he was not there. She walked into the hallway and saw him looking up at the loft hatchway. He tried to reach it, but it was just to far up for him to get to. "I wonder what is up there?" he said as she came up to him.

"Not a lot of old junk, I hope," she said, staring up at it.

"I'll go up there when all the stuff arrives tomorrow."

"I am sure you will. I just hope we will be warm enough here tonight."

"Shared bodily warmth, my dear, the secret to winter survival," He grinned and raised his eyebrows in a mischievous manner.

"It will be a bit spooky though, strange."

"You big wimp" he said jokingly.

"Not me, you daft sod, I am on about the kids."

"Oh, the kids, yeah. Well they will get used to it."

"You think we should all stay together tonight, don't you?"

"No. They have their own rooms and their own sleeping bags."

"Oh come on, Ray, just for tonight. It is very scary for them, you know."

"They have each other, don't they, and they will have to get use to sleeping alone. They're not coming into our room every night, crying."

"I know that, but just for tonight I think we should all sleep together. It is a daunting place for two kids, you know."

"Bloody jam puff, that's who you're on about. I bet Amber will be okay."

"No, she wouldn't, and he is not a puff, stop saying that, please."

"Oh, alright, we will all sleep on the living room floor tonight then. Shall we go and get the stuff out of the car?" He walked away and she followed him, and as they went down the stairs, Diane shouted towards Tommy's room, "Tommy, come and help us get the stuff from the car, darling."

The rest of the day was spent emptying the car and setting up the sleeping arrangements for that night. Each had a sleeping bag and Ray had brought a small heater, which he set up while Diane took the picnic basket she had packed and began to make some sandwiches for their tea. It was not a lot, but at least it gave them something, and with three bottles of pop and crisps with some biscuits they were happy.

Amber was in conversation with Ray about how he was going to do up the small barn for her pony, while Tommy helped his mum. The time passed quickly; the sun began to go down and the warmth of the day began to fade.

The house did not have any central heating, just a fireplace in the main room and one in the kitchen. They had budgeted for double glazing to be fitted in the months to come and were going to relay on heaters for the rooms for now. It was not a decision taken lightly and Diane was not happy at the time, but the heating argument seemed to be resolved at the moment and Ray was happy that it was. And the single light bulb hanging above them was not adequate for the size of the room, but it would suffice for now.

Diane cleared up after their tea and they all sat on the floor in a circle, relaxing for a while in the centre of the large living room.

"Yes, well I have seen where my pony is going to be living," Amber told Tommy with a satisfied smile.

"Have you now, where we going to get the money for that then?"

"I have savings, and anyway, ponies are not that dear."

"Who is going to look after it? Clean out the stall, buy food, pay vet bills, and all the trouble grooming it? You won't," Tommy tells her straight.

"Yes I will, you don't know. I will look after it and ride it and give it anything it needs, so there." She folded her arms and looked at him with her best little madam look, tilting her head to one side cockily.

"Calm down, you two." Diane can see what is coming, she knows her children well enough when to see an argument brewing.

"Tell him then." Amber raises her voice but instantly backs down, knowing she has overstepped her mark.

"I beg your pardon, little lady?" Diane asks, looking at her with annoyance.

"Sorry, Mum" Amber says, bowing her head.

"Yes, I should think so. Now you two can stop all this bickering because it is beginning to get on my nerves, do you both understand?"

"Yes, Mum, sorry." They both submit and the awkward silence which follows is broken by a noise outside, like a cry. They all look up, their fear rising for a moment, but Ray held up his hand, saying with a smile, "Calm down, it is only a fox or cat. You will get used to it."

"A fox? Oh, cool." Amber sits up and listens, trying to hear it again.

"You will hear a lot of noises here that you have not heard before, don't let them bother you. Owls, foxes, cats, birds, and the odd bat flying about as well. We are much closer to nature that you have ever been, so explore it and enjoy it, eh?" He looks at Diane who is listening as intently as her children.

"Wolves?" Tommy asks, raising an eyebrow in disbelief.

"There is not wolves in England, except in zoos. Isn't that right Ray?" Amber announced proudly.

"There are no wolves in England," Diane puts her grammar right with a smile.

"There is nothing here that can harm you if you are sensible and treat everything with respect. You are going to have your eyes opened to nature here, so just be careful and enjoy the big adventure that awaits you." Ray explains.

"Bats get caught up in your hair" Tommy states to everyone.

"No they don't, it's all rubbish that," Diane told him.

"Well if bats are blind, why do they come out at night? What difference does it make?" Tommy asked his mum, who turned to Ray smiling, wanting him to explain.

"They come out at night because what they feed on is nocturnal." He smiled at Diane, who nodded and smiled back at his answer.

The house was locked up and everyone was settled, their sleeping arrangements were agreed on and all were satisfied. The outside of the house was dark and cold looking, the barns were in darkness except for a dim light from the moon and a noise echoes from the small barn.

Beginning with a shuffle, eventually the footsteps scrambled down the ladder and across the floor. Just for a moment, a shadow can be seen, but it disappeared through an opening in the wood at the back of the barn and was gone. Silence returned, everything still and calm.

Only the creatures of the unlit hours moved, the nocturnals, hurrying on their way, doing what they have to do. Finding water, food and in some cases, merely stay alive. Some are harmless, some are hunted and some are hunters; this place as been undisturbed for some time and now that people have moved in, not only do they have to get used to the surroundings, the surroundings have to get used to the new inhabitants as well. Not only the new people that have come to this place, but with new noises, the new routine, the new way of life for some.

As the life outside began for the night, the inside of the house was settling down.

Diane and her children had made sure they had been to the toilet so they don't have to get up during the night. Some of the rooms, including the landing, had no light bulbs at all, so a torch was the best way to see themselves up to the toilet, which none of them fancied having to do on the first night.

The children put their sleeping bags next to each other, Diane put hers next to them and Ray was on the end next to her; he was the last one to settle down and he turned the light out. Although it had been suggested that it be left on, he turned it off anyway.

The children didn't take long to fall asleep, it had been a long day for them and Diane turned to face Ray. The faint moonlight and the fact that her eyes had adjusted to the darkness meant she could see him and she smiled and blew him a kiss.

"Bodie is going to love it here," he said.

"Your precious dog will be here tomorrow, my dear," she said, smiling at him.

"What are you smiling at?"

"You and your dog. If I was the jealous type, I would think that you thought more of that animal than me."

"We have been through a lot together, me and Bodie."

"I bet you have, in fact I bet he could tell me a few tales. You two are much alike, I think. It took him a long time to accept me, didn't it?"

"He will do you no harm."

"I know that now, but you must admit he is a nasty looking dog. Lovely dog, but nasty looking. I nearly shit myself when I first saw him," she rolled her eyes at the thought.

"My best friend Bodie would do anything for me, and me him."

"I was worried about the kids too, to be honest."

"He won't hurt them," he said sincerely.

"What breed is he again?" She shook her head in confusion as she asked.

"He is a cross between a rottweiler and a Leon Berger."

"That is one hell of a cross. He looks like a massive rottweiler."

"He is a big and very strong dog, and he's the best friend I have."

"Oh, I know all about the bond you two have, I learned that very early on. He is very protective of you and he really looks after you, doesn't he?"

"Yes he does and I would do anything for him. You are safe with him about, I tell you. And he is going to love it here."

"I hope we are all going to love it here."

"I'm sure we will," he smiled and winked his eye cheekily.

"Ray, will you tell me something?" her voice was serious and quiet.

"Of course," he said just as serious and quiet.

"Do you like my kids?" she looked at him, keeping her face expressionless.

"What a silly question," he sighed.

"Well you have none of your own. You have never lived with kids and you said you weren't sure in the beginning. Now we're all going to live together and I wondered if you had any doubts. You would tell me, wouldn't you?"

"I have never been a 'kid' person, I told you that, but I try very hard with your kids."

"I don't want you to have to try hard."

"I am on a learning curve. I have never experienced living with kids, I am learning just as we all will, I suppose."

"You will learn a lot, you know. They do love you."

"They put up with me because of you."

"No, not at all, they adore you, really. They love you, do you love them?"

"What has brought all this on? I told you I will try my best with the children, I think we have been okay this past year," he frowned as he spoke.

"Yes I know, I just want everything to be right and go well, I don't want you to regret anything. I love you to bits and I don't ever want to lose you, you're the best thing that has happened to me and I mean that." She smiled at him with warmth and love and he looked back and gave a smile, tilting his head and crossing his eyes to look daft. She laughed and did the same back to him.

"Oh, you are so bloody sexy when you do that," he joked.

She screwed her face up crossed her eyes and jilted out her chin, then said in a moronic voice, "Do you fancy me, will you take me out?"

He threw his head back and laughed, then muffled the sound with his hand. She smiled, she loved to see him laugh, and if she is the one who has made him laugh, then it made her feel good inside too.

"You're a silly sod at times," he said when the laughter had died down.

"That's why you love me," she said, back to her normal self again.

"Well, that and a few other things I can think of"

"And what are they?" she asked, knowing what he was going to say.

He smiled and looked down to where her chest would be if she was not in a sleeping bag. "I'm a sucker for tits, you know that."

"Bloody hell, your tits mad, bloody fed on them and trying to get back on it the rest of your life. Typical man!"

"Oh, I am not 'typical', babe, you know that."

"Yeah, I know that, bloody un-typical."

"Is that a real word? You just made that up."

"Don't be silly because it *is* a real word, you silly sod."

"Well, the fact remains, you have beautiful breasts."

"Breasts? What is wrong with you? What happened to tits, or knockers, or whatever else you usually say? You never say breasts."

"I do try to be polite occasionally," he grinned at her.

"Well, you're not getting anything here tonight, the kids are too close" she said, breaking into a broad smile.

"Bloody spoilsport!"

"All good things come to those who wait."

"Good thing I know they're worth waiting for." He blew her a kiss and they eventually fall off to sleep while the night closed in, embracing the house and farm and all that surrounded it.

CHAPTER 4

The morning was bright and fresh. Ray had been awake and dressed for some time, sitting on the back doorstep, watching the morning arrive. He used to love to do this when he was a child, listening to the night close and the morning open. The sound of birds and animals far away, going about their business, settling in after a night of hunting and surviving, or just awakening to a new day.

He took a deep breath, filling his lungs with the fresh morning air. It felt so good he did it several times, as he stood looking out across the field that spread along the back of his new home. He could just start to hear the hum of traffic way across the field somewhere, as the morning brought out the men and women who were going to work. The noise was ugly to him after experiencing the gentle quiet of the night and break of dawn.

He stretched his arms out and leaned back, yawning. He hadn't gotten much sleep, the floor had been unforgiving and he was a little stiff and sore. And what sleep he did get was disturbed by the dream.

It was always the same. He was always on horseback, always carrying a sword. He felt that he was a warrior, though he never saw who he was slaying. He told himself that it was just a dream, and that it was, although he was always left with an odd feeling of sadness and failure.

It was not long before Diane was awake and then the children, who were sent upstairs with their overnight bags to get washed and ready. She came into the kitchen and, seeing Ray standing just outside the door, she walked over and said, "Good morning. How long you been up?"

"A few hours," he said without turning around. The dream and the feelings were slowly dissipating and he tried to shake them off.

"You should have woken me, we could have had a quickie while the sun came up," she said as she walked out to stand next to him, putting her arms around him and cuddling

him. He put his arm around her, smiling down at her as he did. "What you been looking at?"

she asked.

"I have been listening to the silence and watching the place wake up, beautiful."

"Listening to the silence?" She looked up at him, but he was still looking across the

field as he answered her.

"Yes, it is a beautiful sound if you know how to listen to it."

"Ok, if you say so, babe. Shall I make a drink?"

"Yes, please. What time is it?"

"About six, I think," she said as she went back in, looking for the carton of orange

juice she knew she had somewhere.

"The van should be here soon," Ray said, still standing outside.

"Yes. I hope your mate knows where we are," she says from inside the kitchen.

"He does. And soon Bodie will be here as well." He smiled at the thought.

Diane, shaking her head, still looked in her bags for the orange juice and said nothing

about his dog, keeping the thoughts to herself.

The children came running down the stairs and went out the door to explore the back

and look out into the field. Amber saw herself riding her pony and Tommy was lost with his

thoughts, suddenly Ray was no longer alone, his idyllic morning had been broken. He came

back in and looked at Diane, who smiled back at him.

She was happy and it showed in her face, he smiled back at her as he blew her a kiss,

he liked to see her happy. She winked at him and blew one back. He mouthed the word

'sexy' to her and she nodded, grinning, and mouthed the words 'I know' back to him. He

raised his eyebrows and walked past her, slapping her backside as he did.

He left and went upstairs to the front room, where he looked out the window and down the road that led up to the two front gates. He wanted the van to arrive so he could get started unpacking and getting the beds up, having no desire to spend another night on the floor.

He was anxious to get started, but could do nothing about it until his stuff arrived. Just as he was thinking this he heard his mobile phone ringing downstairs. He dashed down to the front room and took it from his ruck sack. "Hello," is all he said, then just listened.

Diane came in from the kitchen with a glass of orange juice for him in her hand. "Who is it?" she asked as she handed him the glass.

He took it and drank it down in one gulp, giving her the glass right back. "Yeah, that's it, a long narrow road, we're at the top on the right."

"Are they here?" Diane asked, taking the glass.

"Okay, mate. See you in a minute." He put the phone down and turned to Diane with a grin on his face.

"Is he here?" she asked eagerly.

"Just coming up the road," he said. She hugged him and dashed into the kitchen, shouting the children together and telling them what they had to do. Ray went outside and waited at the gates for his friend to bring the large removal van up the narrow road and swing it through the gates, turning it around and reversing closer to the front door where it stopped, shuddering to a halt as he turned the diesel engine off.

The door opened and out jumped a huge dog. It shook itself then spotted Ray, instantly running towards him, wagging its short, stubbed tail. The Rottweiler that was the size of a Leon Berger pounced onto him, knocking him to the ground, and licked him with excitement and affection, feelings which were mutual. Ray was rolling on the ground with his dog and the dog was rolling on the ground with its master, both largely ignored by the small stocky driver as he got out of the van.

He walked past them both and up to Diane, who was smiling at him. He hugged her and kissed her on the cheek, gestures that she returned. He then looked down at the children and put his thumb up, and they did the same to him.

"How are you, Dave?" Diane asked while glancing at Ray, who still play-fighting his dog on the floor, oblivious to their surroundings for the moment.

"I'm fine, love, thanks. This place looks nice," he said as he stood back, admiring the building.

"Would you like a tour before we start? I would offer you a drink, but we have nothing yet."

"Oh, that's okay. I stopped off at a transport café on my way here," Dave said as he was led into the house for a look around. All four of them went in, leaving Ray rubbing his dog's belly as it laid on its back for him. He played with Bodie until they all came back out again, then brushed himself off and came up to his friend, followed by his dog.

"How you doing, ugly bastard?" Dave said to Ray, smiling.

"Better now that our stuff is here. Did you have any problems?"

"No, it all went okay. Bodie whimpered a bit for you last night, but I daren't say anything to him, so I just let him pine." He smiled at Diane who smiled back.

"Shall we get going then?" Ray asked, rubbing his hands together. The rest of that day was spent unloading the large van and getting their belongings into the house. Assembling the beds and making them, connecting the gas cooker, putting in lights and laying down the carpets temporarily. Installing the fridge and freezer, microwave, television, setting up the table and chairs.

The boxes were all marked with what was in them; they had spent a lot of time packing all this two days ago and now were unloading it again. Food and drink, wardrobes, clothes, everything that had to be brought in was; the children's belongings, Diane's things, Ray's things, Bodie's bed and dish.

They all worked hard and were all very tired by the end of the day. Bodie spent his day exploring and marking his new territory, sniffing and investigating everything. Every now and then he would wander into the house, looking for Ray for reassurance, then would go back outside and investigate this new place some more.

Diane organised the proceedings and complained about Ray doing a lot of things, like connecting the cooker. She insisted a professional come and do it, corgi registered, but before she was finished complaining, Ray had done it and tested it by lighting all the gas rings. He couldn't smell gas, so was satisfied with his work, smirking at her as she glared at his cheekiness.

Working hard without stopping, they made good progress. Dave and Ray did a lot of lifting; it was awkward sometimes, going up and down the stairs, but as the day went on they developed a system and methodically got through it.

Finally, the essentials were done. After a long, yet rewarding day, they finally stopped for a break. They offered Dave a bed, but he chose to return home instead. They waved him away and continued working into the night. The kids went to bed, so tired they had no time to be scared or nervous. They were so exhausted and weary that as soon as their heads hit the pillow they were asleep.

Diane made a cup of tea while Ray took Bodie out for a few minutes. Opening the door, he walked out with his companion. The dog sniffed his way around the yard while Ray stretched his aching back. He decided that he was ready for bed and, after watching his dog mark his spot several times, he called him back. Bodie, however, did not come.

He stood rigidly, looking at the small barn with his ears pricked up and his body still and alert. He had heard something and wanted to investigate, but when Ray called him again, he reluctantly returned to his master. He looked back in the direction of the barn as he entered the house, he wanted to go over there. Something was there, he sensed it, but he was told to heel, so he did.

The big dog walked into the house and went to his large basket that had a blanket in it. He was too big for it now and, although he always started his nights off in it, he inevitably was sprawled out on the floor in the morning. Ray petted him and said 'goodnight' to his faithful companion, then went into the main room.

Sitting on the settee waiting for him was Diane. She had a mug of tea in her hand, cupping it with her hands for the warmth. She smiled at Ray with affection as he walked in and sat next to her, picking up the mug of tea that was on the small table next to the settee and taking a sip. He leaned back and sighed, saying, "What a fucking day."

"Language," Diane said, putting him right.

"English," he said smartly, having another drink.

"Yeah it has been busy, hectic and tiring, but it was all worth it in the end. I can't believe how much we got done today."

"Dave was a big help. Good lad, Dave."

"I asked him to stay but he didn't want to. He must be knackered driving back after a day like today, poor sod."

"No, he is as strong as a horse. I bet he won't ache in the morning like we are going to."

"Tired the kids out anyway. They were out like a light, bless 'em."

"Any biscuits?" he asked, looking around for them.

"Oh sorry, I forgot. We have some in the kitchen."

"Suppose I will have to do without then." He sipped his tea, looking at her over the rim of the cup suggestively.

"Would you like me to go and get them for you?" she asked.

"No it's ok, I will do without."

"Oh, bloody men," she said jokingly, standing and going into the kitchen. She reappeared a short time later with a packet of biscuits and threw them at him. He caught them in one hand and opened them quickly. Taking one out, he dipped it in his tea, eating it as she sat back down next to him.

"Thanks, babe, you're a star," he said to her, smiling.

"Well, they're are not too many of us left now, eh?"

"True, true" he took another biscuit and dipped this one in his tea also.

She watched him and slowly shook her head. "I don't get offered one then?"

"Oh sorry, babe, would you like a biscuit?" he said smiling and holding the packet away under guard, not offering it at all.

"No, I won't bother" she took her tea and sipped a little, leaning back as she relaxed her aching body on the settee.

"Bodie loves it here. Shall we go for a walk in the woods tomorrow?"

"Be nice, all of us out as a family. Yeah, be good, that."

"Great place round here, don't you think?"

"Yes, it is very nice. It just worries me that we are off the beaten track and the only way up to us is the one road, though. In winter we might get snowed in."

"Well, you knew that before we bought. They said it was isolated."

"Yes, yes, I know. I do like it, but if one of us needs an ambulance or something in winter, we might have trouble."

"My dear, they have things called helicopters nowadays. You know, the big, bloody noisy things with a rotating blade on top that makes them fly," he said sarcastically, but with a grin on his face.

"If the telephone lines are down, how will they know?"

"If it makes you feel better we will get a short wave radio or something just for emergencies." He takes another biscuit and dunks in in his tea, shaking a little bit of tea off then putting in into his mouth.

"We only have one packet of them, so make them last. At least until we go shopping, that is."

Before he answered, Bodie barked and they both looked up. He was standing by the back door, his nose to the floor. He was getting a scent from the gap under the door and he growled and barked again.

"Bodie, settle down," Ray shouted.

"What's up with him?" Diane asked, looking in the direction of the kitchen.

"He must have heard something, a cat or fox or something. He will settle, he is just not used to the place yet, is he?"

"I hope he doesn't go on all night. Mind you, I'm that tired I think I will fall straight to sleep when I get into bed."

"Spoilsport you are," Ray said with a sly wink of his eye.

"Oh babe, you know I'm not, I'm just too bloody tired." She moved closer to him and snuggled next to him, touching him with her body.

"Sign of old age, that," he said, munching on a biscuit.

"Well you should know." She smiled, taking a sip of her tea.

"Yes, bloody years ago, and I'm still finding out."

She laughed, and looked deep into his eyes, saying, "I never loved anyone like you, I never wanted anyone like you and I never want you out of my life." She had a serious and loving look on her face.

"I know babe, I know," he teased, looking at her with a biscuit hanging out of his mouth.

"I'm being serious, stop messing about," she said as sternly as she could without laughing at him.

He laughed and ate his biscuit, putting the half-empty packet down by the side of the settee. He then finished his tea and put his mug down. Turning serious, he turned and faced her, looking at her with a slightly crooked smile. His blue eyes caused her heart to melt, she always found them sexy and irresistible. It was the first thing she had noticed about him the first time she saw him.

He put his hand on her face, holding her cheek in his palm, and his heat made her heart melt again. "Listen babe," he began in a low, intimate tone, "you know I am not very good at all this stuff, but you do mean the world to me and I am very happy with you. You make me laugh, you make me feel happy and wanted. You are very special and very loving and I don't want to be without you, ever," he said as he leaned forward and kissed her on the cheek.

"Oh baby," she sighed, smiling from ear to ear. "We might just have a quickie tonight when we go up." She winked provocatively.

"Not tonight, darling, I'm just so tired." He touched his forehead with his hand and closed his eyes for a moment before opening them and looking at her, unable to contain a smile.

She punched him playfully and turned away, looking back at him for a moment, but had to look away again because he was smiling at her. She would have to give in, she knew that if she looked into his big, sexy blue eyes or saw his gorgeous smile that she would not be able to resist it. She tried to not look at him, but was conscious he was smiling at her, he was just waiting for her to look round at him.

"Oh, sod it," she said, turning and putting her arms round him. She had to give in and they both knew that she would, at some point.

Again Bodie let out a loud growl. He was unhappy about something and Sasrah, who was trying to keep hold of him, had to let him go because he was pulling away from her so hard. Ray walked into the kitchen with Diane right behind him, while Bodie stood at the back door, alert and listening.

"What is it mate?" Ray asked. Bodie instantly came to stand next to him, looking up at him.

"What's wrong with him?" Diane asked, looking down at the large animal.

"Don't know." Ray knelt down and stroked and petted his dog.

"I'm going up, babe, will you check everything and turn out the lights?" she said.

"Yeah, okay" he replied. After she left the kitchen, Ray went into the living room and turned the light off and when he returned and looked at his dog, he knew something was wrong with him because he was acting so strangely. Kneeling down, he stroked the head of the big, powerful animal.

"What is mate, what have you heard?" He stroked and calmed his dog which sat in front of him, looking up. But Ray knew that he had his mind on the noise he had heard outside. Ray stood and looked at the door while Bodie moved to the door and looked back up at him. He could see in the dog's eyes that he wanted to go out, and wanted to go out now.

"Come on lad, settle down," Ray said masterfully. His dog did as commanded, it rolled up in the basket and dropped his head on his front paws, looking up at his master. Ray looked at the door then back at his dog, finally turning out the light and leaving the kitchen, going to bed.

Bodie listened as his master went upstairs. His ears were pricked up; he knew he was right, he knew something was out there, all he wanted was a chance to go and have a look. But he had been told to lay down and he did as he was told. He knew that something outside was moving away from the house, that it had passed the house on it's way, but after a long period of silence he settled and eventually closed his eyes.

CHAPTER 5

It was loping slowly towards the woods; a little fragile looking thing, more creature than human. It had seen Amber in the shed and it had hidden, but with all these people moving into the house and the dog they had brought with them, it knew life would be more difficult.

The moon light reflected his shape, the shape of a young boy, nervous and full of anxiety. He had to move and go get food, the hunger in his stomach told him, but he was afraid to move. Dressed in rags, with a leather brown belt round his waist, he ran towards the woods beyond the field.

His belt ordinarily supported an old hammer, which was now held tightly by his right hand, and there were four rusty six-inch nails pushed through holes in the belt at the side opposite the hammer. It resembled a western six-shooter with four bullets, but he was not in the Wild West, he was running towards the dark, quiet woods.

Steadily, at a rhythmic beat, he ran; occasionally, the moonlight filtering through the trees showed his gaunt face, drawn and sad-looking, with teeth sticking out from thin gums, and sucked-in cheeks that gave him a malnourished look. His flesh seemed to just hang on his small bones, his legs were so thin that you would not think they would be able to carry him, but carry him they did, and very well.

He started to pick up his pace and the dirty rags that he wore flapped in the breeze that he created. Between his drawn appearance and his nondescript rage, he was a sight that would scare children and make women scream. He held on to his hammer to stop it from flying about as he ran then he stopped and crouched down. Taking a deep breath, he looked around. He was able to see in the dark and, in spite of the seeming quiet, he was nervous and shaking.

He looked up at the moon and snarled, showing his teeth. Slowly he walked into the woods and bowed down to walking in a crouch, more animal than human. Stealthily he went along his way, off the path and into the undergrowth and, as if by magic. He was gone, hidden, but still moving, blending in perfectly with his surroundings. He was in hunting mode and was hungry.

It was not long before he had his prey spotted. A young fox crouched in the brush, it had heard something but was not sure what it was so it was still, listening and looking. Its ears twitched to any sound of the night, any unusual sound, a sound that should not have been there, but it was too late. With skill and accuracy, the hammer was thrown.

It flew silently through the air, hitting the fox square on the head and knocking it unconscious instantly. As soon as the hammer hit, the thing ran out after his prey with an insane look on his face. An excited laugh left his lips as he reached the fox and looked round, checking to make sure that he was alone.

Something was making him nervous about the woods, but he ignored his instincts, instead picking up his hammer from the side of the animal. He took a rusty nail from his belt and put it in the fox's ear as it lay on its side, then lifted the hammer high up in the air, and hit the nail, driving it through the skull and into the brain of the fox, killing it instantly.

He screeched out a long howl of joy and laughed uncontrollably while picking up his food. Then he put the hammer back on his belt and pulled the nail out, which took all his strength. He licked it clean and put it back into his belt and, taking the dead fox, he was gone again, back into the undergrowth to enjoy his meal for the night.

CHAPTER 6

"I'm telling you, I heard something screaming in the woods," Amber was insisting to her brother as they both sat at the table the next morning. Diane brought some tea to them and they both had a drink, pulling faces at each other without letting their mother see.

"It was just probably a wolf," Tommy said.

"There are no wolves here, Tommy," Diane said from the oven where she was cooking breakfast.

"It was a horrible scream, Mum," Amber told her.

"What was?" asked Ray as he walked into the kitchen and sat at the table, yawning.

"She says she heard a scream last night," Tommy told him.

"Amber, why don't elephants eat penguins?" Ray asks her.

"Because elephants live in Africa and penguins in the Antarctic."

"Yeah, but apart from that."

"Because elephants are not meat eaters, they eat leaves and things."

"Yes, but apart from that." he asked with a sigh, regretting asking the question. He looked up and saw Diane's shoulders shaking as she laughed at the oven, refusing to turn around.

"I don't know," she said.

"Because they can't get the wrappers off." He smiled at her and she stared back without expression.

"I don't get it."

"The biscuit, idiot," Tommy told her.

"I still don't get it," she said, shaking her head in confusion.

"What do you do when an elephant comes through your window?" Ray asked her.

"I don't know," she said.

"Swim."

"Ray, for God's sake!" Diane scolded, looking at him with disgust, while Tommy tried to hide his laugh in his hand.

"I don't get it," Amber said.

"It's just him being rude, darling," Diane told her, making a face at Ray.

Standing, Ray smiled at them all and kissed Diane as he passed, going to find Bodie who was laid in the hall. Bending down, he spent five minutes petting and stroking his dog, then, opening the door, he let him out. He stood in the doorway watching his dog scout about the yard and off down the side as he picked up a scent. "Don't go far, boy" he shouted, then went back in to the smell of scrambled egg and toast.

After breakfast, Diane persuaded her children to go for a walk in the woods. They all got their coats on and set off down the road towards the woods, Bodie in front smelling his way forward but keeping an eye on Ray, who was following. They all walked at a leisurely pace; Diane with her arm tucked around Ray's and the two children walking just in front without much enthusiasm, hardly noticing their surroundings. Bodie was loving it, Ray was loving it, and Diane was loving being with Ray and her children. They turned into the wood from the small road and headed into the trees.

"Tell you what, we will play a game. You go first, Tommy," Ray said, "you have to close your eyes and run as fast as you can into the wood, and see how long it takes before you hit a tree." He grinned at his joke and Amber laughed, but Tommy was not amused. He just plodded on without responding, his head down and his hands in his pockets.

Ray watched Bodie rummage through some undergrowth, then shake some soil off his nose before carrying on. He smiled, at least his dog was having fun and enjoying the adventure.

Slowly the children edged forward and were walking in front of them. Ray looked at the disinterest in Tommy and shook his head and Diane, sensing it, looked at him asking, "What's up?"

"You tell me," he said nodding towards the direction of her son.

"He will be okay."

"Fucking hell, what more does he want? I would have loved it here at his age, no worries, you went out, you were out all day with your mates, fucking hell, all you wanted to do was fight and grow up. What is up with that lad?"

"Yeah, and you had no law suits in those days, nor as many paedophiles or fucking sickos about. You just can't let your kids run free any more, darling, it is a different world now."

"He should be up a tree now, scouting the area, or fighting with Bodie."

"I think Bodie scares him a bit."

"Oh, fucking hell, does anything not scare him?"

"Stop picking on him," she said, pulling at his arm as they walked.

They both looked at Amber as she stood still and listened, then asked, "Listen to that, what is it?"

"It's a bird," Ray said.

"It sounds like an alarm going off." They all listened and agreed it did, but looking up they could see the small bird in the tree making all the noise. Tommy turned and looked at the ground as he walked on, Amber was looking up for more birds to spot.

Ray took a deep breath and smiled. "How lovely to breath fresh air again, what a great place."

"Yes, it is beautiful" Diane said, she loved having everyone who she loved with her, she felt so happy and content, so complete and safe. The sun shone through the trees and the place was calm, tranquil; you could easily lose yourself here, all the smells and feelings a wood brings out, all the emotions and memories of childhood. Looking at Ray she could see he loved this place, he looked so happy and content that she could only smile, proud to walk by his side. His joy highlighted her joy and delight.

It was about fifteen minutes later when Bodie started to act strange. He barked then stopped and growled, but there was nothing there. Tommy came up to his mum and stood with her while Amber stood where she was, about ten feet in front. Ray looked at his dog, seeing him sniff the ground, then back off and sniff the air. He looked confused and agitated.

"Bodie, what is it, lad?" Ray said to his dog who replied with a slight bark before running up to Ray, baffled. He stared up at his master, who knelt down and stroked him.

"What is it, Ray?" Diane asked.

"I'm not sure, he has never acted like this before." As Ray tried to comfort his dog, Tommy took hold of his Mum's hand and whispered up to her so Ray could not hear him.

"Mum, can we go home? I don't like it here."

"Oh, Tommy, that's enough!" Diane replied, annoyed. She looked over to Amber, who was standing still, just watching Bodie, then looked back at Ray, watching as he calmed his dog down. Bodie was better, although it was obvious that something was still bothering him, but what it was they didn't know.

They began to walk again and, as they got deeper into the woods, he seemed to calm even more, staying near Ray the whole time. They walked a big circle, eventually ending back where they started from, out onto the road again.

Bodie was completely fine now and ran off up the road ahead. Amber was holding Diane's hand, Ray was walking free just behind, admiring the scenery, and Tommy was in front wanting to get home to get his games console hooked up to the television in his room.

Ray was the one who spoke and broke the uneasy silence; he spoke up in a voice so they all could hear him from the back, "Beware of the woods and the full moon." He smiled as Diane looked back at him and shook her head, but Amber asked curious.

"Why, what is wrong with it?"

"The forest dwellers live in there and they will have you for supper. They dig people up and dress in their skin."

"Ray, for God's sake, stop it," Diane shouted at him, holding Amber close to her. In spite of her obvious disapproval, he was undeterred.

"Just like Ed Gein used to do. He was a murderer, grave robber and necrophiliac. He used to dress up in the skin of his victims." He stopped abruptly when he saw Diane spin on her heels to face him.

She looked angry, her eyes were wide and her face was red. He just looked at her and took the full force of her annoyance as she shouted at him, "That's enough Ray, for God's sake, you're talking to children! Don't you realise what the hell you are saying, for Christ's sake?"

"Okay, calm down. I was just trying to give them a history lesson on some of the more, interesting and influential people of the past. Without Ed, you would not have had films like Psycho, The Texas Chainsaw Massacre, and quite a few others."

"Well, the world would have been a better place without them, I am sure!" She took hold of Amber and held her close, giving her a comforting hug as they walked. Tommy was walking ahead and trying not to listen; he just wanted to get home and back to his room.

"I will keep my information to myself in future then, shall I?" Ray said, more to himself then to anyone else, but Diane heard him and answered him in the same way, not looking at him.

"Yes, you do that!"

He had a smile on his face which none of them could see, the incident was amusing to him and their reaction was even funnier. He didn't understand her hostility but, what the hell, he didn't understand a lot of things, especially children, which were a mystery to him. He had been trying hard with Diane's kids, although he knew he would never understand them.

He shrugged his shoulders and amused himself by watching Bodie, at least he was enjoying himself; sniffing out new smells and marking his territory, stopping at almost every tree to mark his spot, always looking back to make sure Ray was in sight before moving on. He led his silent humans back to the farm.

The atmosphere was lightened that afternoon when Diane decided to go out. She wanted to do some shopping and call at the school she would be working at on the way back. She talked the kids into going with her so they to could see where their education was to be enhanced over the next few years.

They had not spoken to Ray much after the episode in the woods and Diane found him in the barn with Bodie. She saw him threw a ball across the yard behind the barn for Bodie to chase and bring back and continued watching the two. It was obvious that they were happy to be together, best mates, inseparable, and for a moment she felt a slight pang of jealousy. She shook her head at her silliness and approached them, interrupting their game.

"Can I borrow the car?" she asked.

He turned and reached in his pocket for his keys, holding them out to her and saying, "Please be careful, she is a classic. And don't get lost."

"Well if you had an up-to-date car, it would have a sat nav in it and then I couldn't get lost could I?" She looked at him more closely, her eyes narrowing. "Are you okay?" she asked, concerned.

"Yes, we are fine," he smiled.

"Look, I am sorry for losing it this morning, but you can't scare the kids like that, Ray, they are nervous enough moving here. It is a massive thing in their lives, you know, and talking about monsters in the woods just does not help."

"Yeah, I know. I was only having a bit of fun."

"Well, will you please have a bit more tact in future?"

"Yes, Miss," he said with chagrin, as if he were a young child being corrected. She looked down at Bodie who dropped the ball at Ray's feet, panting. He looked at Ray then over at Diane with a questioning look on his face, making her feel uneasy.

"That bloody dog is half human," she said, turning her eyes back to Ray, who was patting Bodie on the head.

"Best friend I have ever had."

"I thought I was your best friend."

"Well, you are. You know what I mean," he said with an impatient shake of his head.

"I wonder if I do sometimes, love. Anything you want from town? I am going shopping and then up to the school to show the kids where they will be going after the holiday, so you and your best friend will have the place to yourselves for a few hours. I am sure that will make you both happy."

"Oh, give us a kiss and stop being fucking stupid," he said grinning and giving her a wink of his eye. That cheeky smile did the trick again.

"You bastard," she said, coming close to him and kissing him, they held each other tight and kissed again.

When she stepped back, he slapped her behind and said, "Don't forget the dog food and biscuits."

"Oh shut up," she said with a smile as she walked away.

"Be careful with my baby. Don't over-rev her," Ray shouted after her. She just raised her hand without turning back. He looked down at Bodie and smiled, "Just you and me now kid, we have the place to ourselves."

He knelt down and stroked his powerful best friend rubbing behind his ears just as

Bodie liked, while the dog wagged his tail with glee. Ray looked up when he heard the engine of his beloved car start up, then get revved intentionally as it pulled away. He shook his head as he watched them go and, when they were out of sight, he led Bodie back into the house.

"Mum, what did he mean about the forest dwellers?" Tommy asked as they drove down the hill and past the forest they had walked in that morning.

"Oh I told you, love, it is just his sense of humour. There is no such thing, he was just trying to scare you, that's all," she told him as reassuringly as she could.

"Oh, that's alright then." He thought for a moment and then asked, "What about that man he said, Ed something?"

"I don't know, probably made him up too."

"It does not scare me anyway," Amber said proudly, looking out of the window.

"Yes it does Amber, you were shitting yourself!" Tommy told her, forgetting where he was for a moment, then regretting what he had said instantly.

"That's enough now, and watch your language, lad!" Diane told him, looking at him in the mirror.

"Yes, watch your language!" Amber joined her mother in saying.

"And you stop being so bloody cheeky," Diane told her. Tommy smiled and was satisfied that she had gotten told off too, that made it ok. It was bad when it was just him but when she got told too, it evened things out.

Satisfied with that, he looked out of the window as they drove along, watching the trees fly by and the road seemed a blur of blue. He looked up at the sky and then looked as far as he could into the distance over the tree line.

Diane drove carefully and was always conscious about damaging the car. She did not like driving it and would be much more content when she got her own car. This one was too big, too noisy and too powerful for her. It didn't take her long to reach the main road, then, looking and checking twice at the junction, she pulled out and headed towards the town.

It was about a thirty minute drive and, now that she was on a more open and wider road, she settled back into her seat and had got herself used to the car once again. She had driven it before, though not very often, and she was a bit surprised that Ray had let her take it so easily. He would normally have put up a resistance but today it was quite easy. "Maybe he felt guilty about his silly childish antics of the morning," she thought.

She pondered the relationship he had with her children, especially now that they would be living together. Not that she hadn't worried about it from the start, but things had been fine until this morning. Maybe it was just his way of having fun, but he would have to remember that they are children and not one of his mates.

She decided to have a talk to him about it when she got back, he needed educating on the way to talk and interact with children. "That's all, yeah, that's it. He just needs to be educated in the way of children," she said to herself. The thought made her feel better and she suddenly felt more relaxed. Not only did she have to look after her children and teach them the right way to talk and behave, but she had to do it to her boyfriend as well. "Oh well, such is life," she thought.

Smiling, she sped up. The power suddenly didn't feel so threatening but she still kept it well below the speed limit for the road. The last thing she wanted was to damage the car or any cars, and the safety of her children was of paramount importance.

She started to think of what she would get from the shops and how much she should spend. It had been ages since she had gone on a shopping trip and, although this trip was for food and supplies, she might still get a chance to look around a few clothes shops on the way.

Afterwards they would go up to the school to show the kids where they will be going, then home for tea. Having her day worked out made her feel much better inside and she decided that she would sort things out with Ray later. With a bit of work they would all be

fine, she was sure of that, and their life would be wonderful.

CHAPTER 7

Ray knelt on the floor, taking the black compound crossbow out of the box. It had been packed away very carefully, hidden it from the children because he knew it was much to dangerous for them to even try.

Bodie sat watching as his master assembled the lethal weapon, affixing the draw cord, then the rifle scope. He stood on the footrest to draw back the powerful bow and, after affixing the cord, he looked at the compression-moulded fibreglass body proudly.

He looked down at Bodie saying, "Draw weight of one hundred pounds, two hundred yard field of fire and the arrows can travel up to three hundred feet per second. It is a magnificent killing machine, my friend." Reaching down he picked up the seventeen inch long hunting arrows with pointed heads and went outside, followed by Bodie as usual.

Going out to the small barn, he looked down between the barn and the other larger one to its right; at the bottom was a tree that was at least one hundred and fifty yards away. He loaded his bow, pulling the strong cord back and into lock position, and slowly placed an arrow in the groove, knocking it back to be in position for the firing cord.

He then lifted the bow and got it comfortable in his shoulder, closing one eye as he looked through the sight and turned it with his left hand to focus it slightly. Smiling, he gently squeezed the trigger; the arrow left the bow at lighting speed and flew through the air, hitting the tree before anyone watching would even realise that it had left the crossbow. Silent, dangerous and lethal.

Ray lowered the crossbow and looked at Bodie, saying with a smile, "You could do a lot of damage with this, my friend. No one would have a chance, they would never even know it was coming until it hit them, then it would be far too late." He knelt down and petted his dog, then they both walked to the tree. He had a lot of trouble getting the arrow out, but managed it by putting his foot on the tree and pulling with both hands. He had extra strong arrows, the weaker ones would break if you hit trees with them.

He walked back to the house and got his torch, coming back out to hide the bow up into the loft. He looked at the new piping and wiring up there, putting the arrows he had next to the bow, which he had wrapped in a protective blanket.

Glancing around the room, he was pleased. It all looked sound enough, no light coming through the roof so it must be secure, the piping and wiring looked professionally done. Once he was done, he went back down the step ladder that he had used to get up there.

They went outside once again and took a slow, careful look about the place. The large barn loomed, empty and cold looking. The doors were not on it and it was open ended so Bodie went in to mark his spot and investigate as Ray looked around the area, trying to think what he could make it into.

A pit could have been dug and his car driven over it for any work that needed doing, "That's it, a workshop and garage, that's what this place is going. My garage." His own garage with inspection pit, ideal and perfect. He left, consciously doing the calculations for the pit as he did.

"Bodie," he called as he walked over to the smaller barn. Standing in the opening of the barn; as with the larger barn, the gates were missing, but this one had not been cleared like the other one. He noticed the roof was in need of repair and the stone base had moss on it, the damp and weathered boards were noticeable.

He slowly scanned the interior, taking in what he saw; an old bicycle at the rear, an old rusty machine that looked like an old farm machine of some sort. Walking over, he saw it was nothing but scrap now, what used to be a running electrical motor was rusted and corroded on one end. Seeing that it wasn't worth bothering with, he disregarded it, deciding that it was for the skip. Then he looked up and saw the elevated platform above him, he needed a ladder to get up there, which he didn't have, so he scanned the area as best he could from the floor.

Bodie was rummaging in a corner, determined to get at something he had smelt. He dug at the ground, his ears up and his concentration centred. Ray walked over and knelt down, watching his dog dig; he could not see anything, just dirt and muck being thrown about as the large dogs claws ripped the dirt up.

He was struggling with a large piece of earth and Ray pulled at it, helping his friend by lifting the clod of earth up so that Bodie could continue scratching and digging. The dog stopped for a moment and put his nose deep in the hole he had dug, sniffed for a few seconds, then carried on.

Ray scraped the soil back, eventually revealing what Bodie must have scented, a decaying fox. There was no way of telling how long it had been buried there, or by whom, what was of more interest to him was what he saw underneath it.

Another bone, a large thigh bone from the looks of it, a femur. It probably should have shocked him, but it didn't for some reason. He didn't touch it and pulled Bodie off, then, after looking at it for a moment, he calmly kicked the dirt back over their find, reburying it, much to Bodie's dismay. He wanted to see what it was he had dug up, but he respected the decision of his master.

Forgetting about their discovery for the moment, Ray turned around, looking more closely at the junk stacked about. He noticed some wooden shutters resting against the far wall and crossed to them, inspecting them. He had found the latches for them in the house when he had first moved in and thought that were removed and disposed of, but here they were.

The shutters were for the inside of the house; a set of each of the downstairs windows but none for the top. He pulled them out to take a better look at them one by one, finding that they were in need of a bit of paint, but in very good condition all the same.

He spent the next hour or so taking them into the house and hanging them. He had to figure out which one fit which window, but he finally got it right. Once done, he stood back to admire them. They were split, hinged in the middle so they folded back, and he had oiled the hinges and they all worked fine now. He also found, to his delight, that even the clasps to hold them in place against the inside wall when they were not used were still there. He had to retighten the screws holding a few of them in place, but all in all they were nearly perfect.

He closed them and brought the metal bar attached to one of the shutters down, this secured them in place and kept them shut. Two small bolts were at each end of the door, these could be pushed up into holes drilled into the window frame, essentially locking them. They shut out all the light and were quite strong and secure. He smiled to himself, he liked them, but he also knew that Diane would not. Opening the shutter again, he fastened it back into its position on the side of the wall.

He walked through the house and opened the back door, looking out over the field and to the small lake beyond, lost in his thoughts for a moment. Bodie came past him and out into the yard, sniffing the air and then the ground. Ray watched him and smiled, the sight of his dog always brought a grin to his face.

They both stayed there for some time, Ray was not looking at anything in particular, just alternately staring over the field to the lake and watching Bodie exploring. It might have looked strange to some people, but to Ray, it was the most natural thing in the world to be silent, alone with your thoughts.

***

After supper that night Diane was cuddled up with her man on the settee. The kids had gone to bed, Bodie had settled, all the doors were locked and they were in for the evening.

"I am not having them stupid shutter things on my windows, babe," she said.

"You will grow to like them. They have so much character, don't you think?"

"No, they are ugly, old-fashioned and look stupid," she complained.

"They are beautiful, contemporary, and look fantastic."

"Bollocks!"

"No, it's true," he smiled as she looked up at him, annoyed.

"Well I do not like them and would burn them on the fire."

"Just give it a few days and see if they grow on you. You never know, you might get to like them."

"Why the hell should we want shutters on the windows anyway? What are we keeping out, the Creature from the Black Lagoon? Going to rise from the lake, is it? Come on, they're bloody horrible!"

"I wonder if that lake has been dragged?" he said more to himself than to her.

"What you mean? Why should they do that?"

"Oh nothing, no reason."

"It will be better when you get up on that roof and put up the television aerial, then we can watch some mind-numbing telly."

"Yeah, it is on my list to do." He squeezed her tight and she snuggled into him a little bit more. "Is the school okay for you?"

"Yeah. Like I said, it looks okay. The kids were a bit dubious, but it is all new and scary for them at first, isn't it? A bit daunting?"

"Best thing to do is find the bully and go and smash his face in, then you're left alone by everyone from that day on."

"Well, we're not all like you, darling. Tommy is not like that, is he? Although I'm not sure about Amber. Anyway, I don't want my kids fighting at school, they go there for an education not a fight."

"He will be bullied if he does not stick up for himself."

"He will be okay, don't worry about him."

They both look up and listen as they hear someone come down the stairs. The door opens a moment later and Tommy is standing there in his pyjamas. He looks at Ray and gives a false smile, then turns to his mum, saying sheepishly, "Mum I can't get to sleep. It's scary in the dark."

"Don't be silly, it's only you who is making it scary. It's the same at night as it is in the day, it's just your imagination that makes it scary."

Diane smiled at Ray and stood, taking Tommy back to his room. Ray shook his head in disbelief and disgust, then he got up and walked to the kitchen to put the kettle on. Looking down at Bodie, who was curled up on his large blanket, he said, "He can't sleep, so mummy has to tell him a story, no doubt."

Bodie looked at him without reacting. He is concentrating on a noise from outside he had noticed for the past half hour. He notices a lot of noises here, but this one is different, not like the rest. More human, but not totally, and it confuses him a little.

Ray made the tea and walked back into the room, sitting down to wait for Diane to return. Handing her the cup as she sits down next to him a short time later, she cups it in both hands and takes a sip. "Thanks, nice to know you have some uses," she joked.

"All settled in, is he? What's up with him?"

"He can't sleep."

"Tell him to have a wank and release sleep hormones. He will drop off then."

"What?" she says, almost dropping her tea, "is that what you do?"

"No, don't be silly. But it is a fact that when a man or boy ejaculates, he releases sleep hormones. That is why a lot of men roll over and go to sleep after sex, you women just don't know these things."

"What a load of shit!" She looked at him straight in the eye with a little grin on her face.

He looked back as seriously as he could and replied, "It is true, give him a towel or something so he does not mess the sheets, and he will drop off after it with no problem."

"Oh, stop it, stop it," she said, shaking her head, "it's my little boy you're talking about."

"You can't sit there and be in denial, it will happen; in fact I bet he does it already."

"I'm not listening. He is my baby, stop it." She does not want to hear it, although deep down she knows it is probably true.

"You will be shuffling his sheets instead of folding them soon" Ray said.

She punched him playfully on the arm and he flicked her on the nose. Putting her cup down, she jumped on him and they play-fought on the settee like two little kids. They continued fighting for a while until he used his strength to pin her and sit on top of her.

Taking her wrists in his powerful hand, he secured them above her head and, with his free hand, he undid her blouse, one button at a time. She stopped resisting and they kissed passionately on the lips while he cupped her breast and squeezed. She responded with a moan and threw her arms around his neck, pulling him into her, wrapping her legs around him.

They had sex there on the settee and later retired to bed and made love. Diane had always told him there is a difference, not that he noticed, he thought that both were fantastic.

Tommy can hear the noise; he knows what they're doing and sometimes puts his head under his pillow, but he cannot sleep tonight anyway, he does not feel safe here. He does not like the place, something about it disturbs him. He picked up his mobile phone and began to flip through texts he had gotten from his friends when he noticed his battery was very low. They still hadn't found his charger so he turns it off, making a mental note to try and find it tomorrow.

He heard a noise from outside and jumped at it. It sounded like a shriek, probably a fox. He does not like this place, he much preferred their own house. Then too, he preferred it when there was just his mum and his sister, although he had warmed to Ray over the last year.

Now, though, he was becoming a little resentful of him. Ray took a lot of his mother's time and he wanted his mother now, needed that closeness. He seemed not to get it much and Ray had it all, in his eyes. It was not fair, she was his mother after all.

Before, he only saw Ray every other weekend and some holidays. But now he was to be with them all the time and he had to start a new school; he left all his friends and would have to make some new ones.

He hated it here, he didn't see why they had to come here. He even wondered if he could go and live with his dad, but he knew this was impossible. His dad had no room and his mum would never allow it anyway. He knew he was stuck here, but he didn't like it; he felt trapped and felt it so unfair he had to live in this place.

***

"Well, where did you see it last?" Diane asked as Amber ate her cereal the next morning while sitting at the table in her pyjamas.

"At home. I put it in one of the boxes," she said with half a mouthful of corn flakes, munching as she spoke.

"Don't talk with your mouth full, love."

"Yeah, and my charger is missing, Mum." Tommy added.

"Oh, bloody hell, it will turn up. We still have a few more boxes to open, I'm sure they will be in there. Okay?"

All three nodded at each other in some sort of silent code, then finished eating in silence. Diane looked over at Bodie who was standing by the back door, listening to something. She got up and opened it for him and he dashed out and went round to the barns. Coming back, she sat back down and took her cup of tea and started to sip from it, watching her children finish their breakfast.

Ray entered smiling. He patted Amber on the head and toy-punched Tommy on the shoulder as he sat down.

"That hurt," Tommy complained, rubbing his arm.

"Oh, stop being a big puff," Ray told him, pouring himself some tea from the tea pot.

"Yeah, you big puff," Amber spouted up.

"That's enough!" Diane commanded to them all.

"Amber, a scientist has invented a bra that stops tits from bouncing up and down and nipples sticking out in the cold; his colleagues have kicked the shit out of him," said Ray, matter of factly.

"I don't get it," she replied, with a confused look on her face.

"He is just being dirty, Amber, ignore him," Diane told her.

"Okay," she agreed and carried on having a drink of her orange juice.

"We are going to have to look for Amber's phone today, and Tommy's charger. They seem to have lost them," Diane told Ray across the table.

"Have you looked in the couple of boxes that we have not unpacked yet?"

"No, we are going to do that today."

"Where is my boy?" he asked, looking into the kitchen for Bodie.

"I let him out, he was standing by the door. Are you going to sort out the phone today, we need to ring them and get someone to come out and give us a quote or something."

"Yeah," he replied distractedly. "I am going to put my picture up today, in the hallway."

"Shouldn't we decorate first, babe?"

"The picture can come down when we decorate. It has to go up as a mark of respect to the heroes who gave there lives for us, darling," he said sincerely.

"It's only a stupid war plane," Tommy said disrespectfully.

"A what? It's a Hawker Hurricane, son, the work horse of the battle of Britain."

"Battle of what?" Amber asked.

"Britain, love, the Battle of Britain, when fighter command stood alone against the might of the German Air Force. Without the courage and sacrifice of those men, we would not be here now, and the world would be a very different place."

"Okay, calm down, Ray, it is only a plane," Tommy insisted.

"A what? Don't they teach you lot anything in schools today? What a bloody disgrace, what the hell is happening to the world?" Ray said, his voice raising.

"They're too young to understand, babe," Diane said in their defence.

"Well they should be taught to remember and respect their past, to remember the sacrifices people made for them and the hardships that were endured to secure their future, all of our future's. That is what is bloody wrong with today, people just forget and, what is more disturbing, they are allowed to forget. It should be taught in our schools with pride."

"What has a stupid plane got to do with that anyway," Tommy challenged. Diane could see something brewing and was about to step in, but Ray held up his hand and looked at Tommy face on.

"That stupid plane, together with the Spitfire and the courage and skill and sheer balls of the pilots who flew them, kept Hitler from invading our land, son! He needed air supremacy before he could form an assault, the only thing stopping him was a handful of planes and pilots. At one time every plane we had, every single plane, was up in the air, no reserves, no back-up, not anything. It was all or nothing."

"So? What has that got to do with me? They were getting paid."

"Getting paid?" Ray's blood was boiling but he kept calm for the moment, and tried to explain his point once again. "Do you understand what the hell it would have been like in one of those planes, son? Have you any idea what the hell they went through? You're travelling at hundreds of miles per hour; look, just imagine you are in a car travelling at one hundred miles a hour, okay? All your friends cars are blue, all the enemy cars are red and you have to travel at speed and not hit any other car. But things are going so fast that you have no idea, a lot of the time, who are friendly and who are not, and it's not just in a straight line, you're all over the place.

"All the red cars are firing at you and you have tremendous G-force going on as you manoeuvre your plane. It's bloody terrifying. Now increase that by about ten and you might have some idea what the fear factor might have been for those young lads. You have no idea what that sort of fear is like and I hope you never do, but you have to respect the men and women who gave their lives for us in the war, son. 'There is no greater quality in a man than courage,' Winston Churchill said that."

"Who is Winston Churchill?" Amber asked.

Ray rolled his eyes, he just did not understand why these children knew nothing of the war or people like Winston Churchill. He looked at Diane for help before he exploded.

"Winston Churchill, love, was the prime minister of this country when we were at war with Germany," she told her.

"Why were we at war anyway?" she asks naively.

"Because on the first of September, nineteen thirty-nine, they invaded Poland and threatened to take over the whole of Europe by force and put it under German rule," Ray told her.

"Germany makes better stuff than us anyway, like cars and stuff," Tommy said, seeing that he was annoying Ray. He felt he could get the upper hand here and didn't want to lose the chance.

"Imagine that we were at war now, son, and your mother had to go and fight. Imagine that she gave her life and was killed fighting to give you a safe future and somewhere you could live free, in a Democracy and not somewhere where you're ruled by an iron fist. What if then you have children and they say, 'well, so what,' would that make you feel good, knowing that they do not appreciate the sacrifice she had made for you and them?"

"There isn't a war, and she would not go anyway, you don't have to go."

"Of course you have to fucking go, you stupid sod, you got put in prison if you don't. It just disgusts me that you are so unappreciative of the whole thing. If it was not for these people you would not be here and your mum would not be here. They won the war so you could have the life you have, free and able to do anything you want. They should be remembered and honoured."

"Well I don't agree. I think war is stupid, and I think war planes are stupid."

"Okay, that's enough. Let us all just agree to disagree, shall we?" Diane says to them all with authority, she wants to defuse the situation right away.

"I think it is a nice plane, Ray," Amber tells him, putting her hand on his arm as if to calm him and give him comfort and support.

"Yes, Amber, it is. I'm glad that someone has the brains to appreciate it. Thank you." he says to her, taking a drink of his tea and looking at Diane.

There is an uneasy silence until Tommy finishes his drink and leaves the table, walking out of the room. Diane watched him go, then looked back at Ray, who was staring at her, ready for her to speak.

"Don't be too harsh on them, babe. Not everyone has the same opinion, do they? It's not their fault."

"No fucking respect, that is the problem. No respect for people now, or people in the past. Why are they not taught this stuff in schools?"

"Well, if you are going to swear, I am going to get dressed," Amber said with a smile, calmly walking out the room and going upstairs.

"Make sure you have a wash and brush your teeth," Diane shouts after her. Turning back to Ray, she just sits and looks at him. He is annoyed and she wants to ease the tension, so she calmly says as she sups her tea, "My fanny isn't half sore this morning."

"Yeah, my cock aches as well," he says, smiling slightly back at her, she smiles at him and reaches across the table, rubbing his head like she would one of her kids. He pulled away, holding his fist up in a playful manner.

"Don't let them bother you, babe, they're only kids."

"If I had back-chatted my dad like that, he would have put me through the wall."

"Well, times change, sweetheart. It doesn't matter if you're his dad or not, that is the way kids are nowadays. He is going through the change, isn't he? All his hormones are mixed up and his body is changing, it happens to us all, even you. I bet you were a right little sod when you were his age."

"I did what I did, but I always had respect. What the fuck do they teach them at school these days?"

"Everyone is different, not everyone is interested in the past."

"It's not just about that, is it? The younger generation should not forget the older one that gave all they had, all of their sacrifices and suffering."

"I know, I know. Come on, give us a kiss," she said, winking at him. He leaned over and gave her a kiss on the lips, but pulled away when he heard Bodie barking outside. Getting up, he walked to the back door, looking for his dog.

"Do you want some breakfast, love?" Diane asked.

"No, I'm okay, babe," Ray said before walking out and around to the front yard. Listening to Bodie's barking, he followed the sound, finding him in the small barn, staring and growling up at the platform as Ray entered. "What have you seen, lad?" he asked, coming and kneeling down to stroke the large head of his best friend. Looking up towards the

platform Ray sees nothing, but his dog knows differently. He knows that something is up

there.

CHAPTER 8

Diane was washing up and clearing the kitchen table when both Ray and Bodie come back in. Ray put fresh water and some food down for his dog, then came back into the kitchen and snuck up behind Diane, who was at the sink washing the cereal bowls, wrapping his arms around her and giving her a squeeze.

"What's up with him?" she asked.

"Just a rabbit or something, I think." He kissed the nape of her neck and she lifted her shoulders, smiling. She loved it when he did this, and it always sends a shiver down her back. She turned her head and kissed him.

"Mummy, tell him to let me in the bath room," Amber shouted from upstairs.

"Tommy, let her in the bathroom," she bellowed, while Ray pulled away holding his ear.

"Bloody hell, woman."

"Oh, sorry, love," she laughed and smiled at him.

"What about stripping the walls today. Ready for a lick of paint?"

"Can we get the kids rooms done first, it will make them feel more at ease I think. Then the main room and the kitchen. I brought a colour chart from the shops yesterday, we will pick some colours today and start to sort the place out. We have loads to do before school starts."

"I have to go into town and start looking for work too, of course there's not a lot of work for my profession, balloon blower-upper. It's not bad at Christmas, but it dies off as the year goes on."

"What the hell you talking about?" she asks, not really listening to him.

"Nothing important. We will start the decorating today and get a move on with things then, shall we? We will start by empting the boxes that are left, I know I have some stripper and decorating tools in there. If we all muck in, we will soon get the place looking like home, don't you agree?"

"Yeah, that will be good. Exciting, isn't it?"

"Bloody ecstatic, I must say," he mumbled.

"What are we going to do about the flooring? We have to decide on what is getting carpeted and what is going to get laminated."

"One thing at a time, babe. We will get the walls done first, then the floor can come later, okay? Look at it with a man's logic, please, not a woman's."

"Oh, very funny."

"All the mess you will make decorating the walls and ceilings will make a mess of your floor, so we do all the messy stuff first then the floorings go down last thing. Simple logic," he said, smiling smugly.

"We have to give the kids things to do, something to occupy their minds and keep them interested. They will get bored easily."

"Well, tough, they will have to muck in and help. Many hands make light work."

"They will, and it will be good for them to choose what they want in their rooms. Come on, I just want to get started now, don't you?" She sounded like a child with a new toy, all smiles and enthusiasm.

"Lets work on it logically then, one room at a time don't you think?"

"We will get under each others feet. Why not split in two groups and do a room each? What does man's logic say to that?"

"Man's logic says that the woman is getting too cheeky and needs a slap of arse."

"Well, when man is big enough, maybe he will get the chance."

She laughed at him and turned away, Ray then grabbed her from behind and slapped her rear with his hand. She screamed out and struggled, but he had her tight so she took it like a woman.

The next few days were very busy. They stripped all the walls and sorted out the décor, the children's rooms were painted and Diane was right, they enjoyed having a say in what colour scheme they could have.

Tommy picked a deep red and Amber picked a light pink and red, neither to Ray's taste, but he said nothing. Heaters were placed in the rooms and arranged how they wanted them, all that was needed now was the carpet, which Ray went and fetched while they started on the living room. All three of them stripped the walls, while Ray laid the carpets in the rooms that they had finished up stairs.

The children were a lot happier in their rooms, they felt safer and more at home, the chargers and phone still had not been found and were presumed lost. They had promised to be bought new soon but for now they had to do without, which did not go down very well at first, though they soon come to terms with it. It might have had something to do with their being kept so busy with things to do. Diane knew how to handle them and manipulate them in a good way, one that Ray had yet to figure out.

Ray still had not sorted out the phone line, there was a some delay and they said it might be weeks. This did not please Diane, but she to accepted it, just as she had finally accepted the shutters on the windows. She had painted them and made them look a lot nicer, but she knew that the first chance she got, they were going. As far as she was concerned they were only a temporary feature.

Ray did get around to putting the television aerial up, climbing up the cast iron drain pipe at the back to get onto the roof, much to Diane's unease. It didn't take him long to strap and secure the pole to the chimney mast then the aerial to this, feeding the wire down the roof and tacking it down the outside wall and into the house through a hole in the window sill. It was a momentous occasion that night when they all sat down and watched television together.

Within only a matter of a few weeks, the place was nearly how they wanted it. Although the money was running out and their savings were going down, they had a lot to show for it. All the rooms were now done, all the floor coverings down, fittings and fixtures how they wanted them, heaters where they needed them; it looked and felt much more like home.

The kids were more at ease and seemed to sleep better, although with the pace their mother made them keep, they were tired every night from exhaustion and hard work. She didn't let them slack at all, everyone pulled their weight and got the job done. The only thing that had fallen down, in her mind, was the phone.

There was still no sign of getting the line connected yet and she had made the decision to go in herself the next time she was in town. She had seen their shop many times and now it was time for action. Phoning was no good, they only had Ray's mobile at this time and she felt she wanted more; she would feel safer with a phone line in and a working phone. She wanted new mobiles for them all, but the money just did not stretch to it at this time.

The house felt warm and safe at last. She was becoming so happy and content that sometimes when she looked around, she had to pinch herself to make sure it was all real and really hers. The place was lovely and she knew she would be happy here, she had all she wanted and all she needed. Her sights were on her new job now, and soon it would be time to go and start that.

The kids were starting the same school and they were a bit anxious about that but that was to be expected, she told herself. All that was needed now was to get Ray a job and then they could go on living the rest of their lives together here in their beautiful house, together just like a real family.

***

It was dark when she pulled in and past the gates, she had been out all day looking at shops and had come back late. It was dark and the place looked so much more mysterious in the dark, not to mention the fact that her eyes were heavy because she was tired. She turned the wheel and drove up to the front of the house, suddenly shaking with fright. She froze and slammed on the brakes.

A figure, yes, definitely a figure, had ran across the beam of the headlights. For a moment she did not know what to do, her heart beat faster, she was hyperventilating and her fear had incapacitated her for a moment.

She swallowed and looked into the darkness. She knew it had run towards the barns so she slowly drove around and turned the car to face them. Switching to full beam, she looked out across the yard to the barns. She could see nothing now, she strained her eyes as she searched the projection of light from the cars lamps.

Shaking her head she turned and drove back to the front door, still trembling. She hit the horn twice and waited, then she did it again and waited again, heaving a sigh of relief when the light came on and the door opened. Ray stood there looking out at her with Bodie was behind him. She got out of the car and locked it up quickly, rushing past Ray to get inside, she turned and locked the door.

"What the hell's up with you?" he asked, seeing her nervous state.

"Oh fuck, I think there is someone out there!"

"What do you mean, have you been followed?"

"No I was pulling in and something ran across the headlight beam."

"Probably a fox."

"It wasn't a fucking fox, it was a man or something. Someone is out there on the grounds and he ran to the barns. I told you that we needed security lights up."

"Calm down, babe. You saw a man run across to the barns? Are you sure it was a man, did you see him properly?"

"No, I didn't fucking see him properly. It was so fast, it just ran across the front of the car. A small man or something."

He put both his hands on her shoulders, and then spoke to her firmly but calmly. "Or something?"

"Yes, something. Let the dog out, where is he?" she frantically looked past Ray for Bodie.

"Hold on, babe, hold on, calm down. He went out earlier."

"Well let him out again. Bodie," she called, pushing the bewildered dog out the door when he came, then shutting it again quickly behind him. She looked at Ray with fear in her eyes, he could see she was very shaken up.

"Go make a cuppa, babe. I will go and have a look outside," he said as he walked with her to the kitchen. He reached under the sink and brought out a torch, turning it on to see if the beam was powerful enough, which it was. He smiled at her and she smiled weakly back at him, still shaking.

"Be careful, please be careful," she said. He nodded without saying anything then left. She watched him leave the kitchen and then heard the front door open and close. He was gone, out into the night. She stood there for a moment, just listening, although she did not know what for.

Looking around she decided to make a drink, she noticed her hands shaking as she picked the electric kettle up to fill it from the tap at the sink. Swallowing hard because her mouth was dry, she tried to calm herself. Maybe it was just a fox after all, she is tired and may be the night light was playing tricks on her?

She finished making the tea and took two mugs into the front room. A shiver ran up her spine, as though someone had just walked over her grave, she thought. She looked around the room nervously and put the mugs of tea down on the small table next to the sofa. She jumped when she heard the front door open. Bodie came in first, wagging his tail, and came

up to her. She petted him but was not looking at him, she was looking at the door, waiting for

Ray to come in, which he did a minute later.

He looked down at her and smiled as she asked eagerly, "Did you see anyone?"

"No, nothing, no one there, darling. Bodie had a sniff about but there is no one there,

we looked out in the barns and all around the house."

"I did see something, I am not making it up," she said in defence.

Ray gestured to Bodie to leave the room, which he did without question, going back to

the kitchen to his bed. Sitting next to her, Ray took a mug of tea and drank a little, then,

holding it in his hand, he looked at Diane and said calmly, "You are safe here, don't worry."

"Have you locked the door?"

"Yes, we are secure."

"I want some security lights put up outside," she said firmly.

"Well we can do that, but they will be triggered off by cats, foxes and God knows

what else during the night, won't they?" he said, composed and laid back.

"You don't believe me, do you?"

Her voice was challenging and Ray did not like it, he looked her straight in the eye

and spoke in a tone that he usually reserved for the children, "Yes, I do believe you that you

saw something, but what it was is the question here. If it was a man, then surely we would

have found him or at least seen some sign of him."

"I hope you are not patronising me, I am not a fucking child!" She turned away from

his gaze and stared at the wall opposite.

"No, I am not patronising you." His voice was back to its normal tone, and this alone

made her turn back. She looked him in the face, studying him for a moment, then his stern

expression broke and he winked and smiled. She looked away again, trying to hide her grin, he had done it again, that bloody smile of his got her every time.

"You sexy bastard," she said under her breath but loud enough for him to hear. He put his hand on her shoulder and gently pulled her towards him, she came with ease and put her arms round him.

"Probably just an animal or something, darling," he said comfortingly.

"Yeah, maybe." She was not convinced but decided to let it go. She felt now felt safe and warm in his arms; the world outside did not matter at this moment in time, no matter what was out there.

"I am going to get the biscuits, won't be minute," he said and she releases him and holds his tea for him while he disappeared into the kitchen. He knelt next to Bodie, rubbing the dog's ears with both hands. He winked at him as a friend would, then smiled, it was almost as if they knew something that no one else knew and it was their secret to keep.

The dog responded with a lick on his hand and a wagging tail and, after a few moments, he stood and took a packet of coconut biscuits from the cupboard, returning to the front room. He sat next to Diane, both of them getting into a position they have been in a hundred times before; both close, both having a drink and Ray devouring a packet of biscuits.

"Bet you think I am a right idiot, don't you?" she said, looking into the mug of weak tea that she was holding in her right hand.

"No, not at all. It must have given you quite a fright, darling."

"It bloody did, I nearly shit myself. Something ran across the lights of the car."

"Well, there's nothing there now and we are safely locked in."

"Good, and I'm going to get the fucking telephone sorted tomorrow. I am sick and tired of waiting now, they're bloody useless."

"Good idea, and while you are at it go and see why the dustbins are not getting emptied. I am going to have to go to the rubbish tip again this week."

"It's like no one wants to come here. Why is that do you think that is?" she asked him with a curious frown on her face.

"No, it's not that, it is just the incompetence of the lazy fuckers. Because we're off the beaten track, they can't be bothered."

"Yeah, but we have been here for weeks now and no one has been near. No post, no telephone company, no one, not even a visit from the neighbouring houses. It is a little far away, fair enough, but you think someone would come and say hello."

"Sod em, I like it. I prefer being left alone."

"That may be, my love, but you are living with two children now and they like to have friends, kids to invite over to play."

"They will get all that shit when they go to school. No one knows us, do they?"

"I suppose." She wonders for a moment, then looks up saying, "it's not all that shit anyway, they need friends."

"The way Tommy acts, I think a friend would scare him to death," Ray said flippantly, shaking his head.

"Oh leave him alone. You're always picking on him," she spouted up in her child's defence.

"No, I am not always picking on him. I just think he is going to have to let go of your apron strings because there is a big bad world out there and if he doesn't toughen up, it will break him in to little pieces."

"He will be okay, don't worry. It is just all new and they have to find their feet, I told you all this. You need patience with children, Ray, a lot of it."

"Okay, but don't say I didn't warn you. I was out and ready for the world at his age, I had to be. Fight or flight where I come from, if I came in crying because I lost a fight my dad would tan my arse and send me back out to get the lad. Bloody hell, I could never lose a fight, I was more worried what my dad would do to me if I did. You have to stick up for yourself, it's the only way."

"That was when you were young, babe. Times change."

"Nothing changes. You are still victimised if you don't stick up for yourself, still picked on if you are weak. Nothing changes, in fact, it gets worse." He took two biscuits from the packet and dipped them into his tea before eating them both together in one go.

"You can't go through life thinking everyone is out to get you, surely."

"I am not saying that, but until you know you must be on your guard. Ready, switched on. I mean, look at that fucking arsehole a few week ago at the train station, hitting that old man. It fucking made my blood boil that, I could have kicked shit out of that wanker and I would have enjoyed it."

"It was wrong, yes, and it was horrible what they did, but you didn't have to get involved. Was it any of your business?"

"What?" He was astonished that she had said that and he put his mug down and his packet of biscuits also, turning to face her straight on. "Are you serious? What the hell was I supposed to do, just watch a few total wankers kick the living daylights out of an old lad? He probably fought in the war to make the country free and safe for bastards like that, and that is the thanks he gets? It is a fucking disgrace, the whole country is becoming a disgrace." He was annoyed and it was obvious by the sound of his raised voice. She wanted to smile but dared not, she saw how serious he was.

She looked at him expressionlessly and nodded, agreeing with him. "Yes, it was not right. In a way, it was a good job that you were there."

"Yes it was. Most other spineless bastards would have said nothing and just let them get away with it." He calmed down and reached back down for his tea and biscuits, taking a long drink from his mug.

"Are you ok? You will give yourself an ulcer one day, you are going to have to learn to calm down a bit."

Oh fuck it, some people just piss me off, and twats like them on the train platform are just the ones I mean. This society is just too easy, there are no deterrents. I would not have dreamed of hitting an old man when I was young, another bloke or someone you were in a fight with, fair enough, but I never went out looking for it and I would always respect my elders. That is the trouble with the youth of today, no fucking respect."

"You won't change it, darling, it is how life is now."

"Bollocks! I do not have to accept it."

"Yes you do. The law says what is right and wrong. You will eventually have to come to terms with it, we don't live in your era any more."

"The law is bollocks, they do nothing but protect the criminal. Being law abiding is rubbish, you are abused and shit on. I know someone who got sent to prison for kicking a lad to death on the street. He was given a minimum sentence for manslaughter and while he was in jail, he was given free training and got a licence to drive J C B diggers while he was in there. When they let him out, he got a job on the fucking gas board, driving diggers and making fucking shitloads of money. He was given preference because he was coming out of prison!

"It is a bloody shame, any law abiding person would have had to pay for the digger licence himself and would not of been given preference for the job. It's like fucking drug users, they are given everything they fucking want; housing, allowance, the fucking lot, and they get away with shoplifting, mugging, stealing and God knows what else because they are under the influence of drugs. Well fuck it, that's what I say. "They should be banged up in a six by four cell and fed on bread and water for six months, that would bloody cure them."

He took two more biscuits and dunked them in his tea before eating them, then drank down the last bit of tea he had left in his mug.

"Can we change the subject, please? I don't know what got us on to all this in the first place," Diane said.

"I can't help it, it fucks me off. I was telling Tommy last week that bloody TB is back in the country. We got rid of that, so where is it coming from? Bloody immigrants, that is where, bringing all sorts of fucking diseases in to our country."

"Can you stop talking to the kids like that Ray? They are very impressionable and will go into school talking like that."

"That is just my point, we do not have freedom of speech in this country. If I say something, it is racist, but an immigrant says something, it is his right and his freedom of his own opinion. He is okay to incite anything and it is his right, human rights and all that bollocks. But I say it, oh no, you are a racist. Well fuck them all, we should send the fucking lot back where they came from."

"Calm down, darling, you are scaring me." She faced him and could see the anger in his eyes and face, he was tense and his teeth were clenched. Shaking his head, he sat up straight before he carried on with his views.

"We are second class citizens in our own country, I mean they said it was racist to put up a Union Jack not too long ago. What a load of fucking bollocks! You tell me another country that would put up with that. What would they do in America if someone said don't fly the Stars and Stripes, would we find it racist? Let's just get real.

"It makes me sick to think this country is broken, gone down the tubes. Immigrants and God knows who else come here get free handouts, free medicine, anything they want. They never pay into the system and the bloody taxpayer has to foot the bill for it. Those politicians want to get in the real world, if they had a load of them living next door, if they had money taken out of their pockets and were treated like second class citizens in their own country, they would change their minds. It is a fucking travesty."

"Hey, come on, calm down. You are working yourself up, babe. We're okay here, aren't we? We are going to have good life."

He ignores her, or chooses not to hear, and carries on, "It's like if some fucker breaks into your house, you are not allowed to touch them. What the fuck are you supposed to do, tell them, 'Oh, it's okay, just take what you want'?" Fuck that, that is just what I mean, no deterrents. They get away with it, so they do it all the more.

"You stole a car, caused thousands of pounds of damage, caused upset and expense to the car owner? Please don't do it again, here, we will send you away skiing for a week. It is a fucking joke! If any fucker touches my car I will break their legs, if any fucker comes in here I will break their back. If you can put a sign up saying beware of the dog, enter at your own risk then why can't I put a sign up saying if you enter here uninvited, you will be smashed with a baseball bat?"

"Ray, please, just calm down." She frowned and looked worriedly at him, she then held him by the arms and stared at him while he looked at her with hate in his eyes. His neck was red and his veins were bulging, suddenly it all seemed to turn off and he was back to his normal self.

He smiled and quietly said to her, "Just expressing my right to freedom of speech."

"You looked evil then, babe, horrible. I've not seen you like that before."

"Well it pisses me off. It is supposed to be our country and you just see it having its back broken and no fucker seems to be bothered."

"Are you okay? The worried tone in her voice was apparent.

"Yes, I'm fine, are you okay?" he smiled and seemed to be the old Ray that she knew and loved again. Her thoughts were running away with her, she always knew he could have a temper, but he had never directed it at her. She knew he was very opinionated at times, but he just seemed another person there for a moment, smiling, she disregarded it, put it to the back

of her mind. She did not want anything to go wrong and hoped it was just an isolated

incident.

She drank her remaining tea and put the mug down on the floor then settled back into

the settee and stretched, noticing that her body was aching and she was tired.

"Shall we go to bed?" she asked and it seemed to bring on a yawn. She could not help

herself but it felt good, she liked a good yawn.

"No, I am going to stay up a little while, babe. There is a documentary on tonight

about Peter, I want to watch that."

"Peter who? Why don't you just record it and watch it tomorrow?"

"Sutcliffe, the Yorkshire Ripper. Born second of June, nineteen forty-six, in Bingley,

West Yorkshire. In nineteen eighty-one he was convicted of murdering thirteen women in the

north of England. In fact, he attacked more. He attacked one in my home town, you know,

years before. I remember all the hype going on when he was at large."

"Ray, sweetheart, you have a morbid fascination with very strange things and people.

If you know all about him and that, why are you watching a documentary about him on the

television?"

"It interests me, you know it does."

"Yes, I know you like all things weird, but it worries me sometimes."

"Oh, stop moaning. And if you are awake when I come up, I will take you over my

knee and give you a nice spanking."

"Oh? Is that a threat or a promise?" she asked, giving him a cheeky school-girl smile.

Then, standing, she bent down and kissed him.

He returned her gesture of love, then slapped her behind as she turned to walk out the

room, telling her, "You're a kinky cow, do you know that?"

"That's why you love me, isn't it?" she says as she leaves the room. Looking at Bodie as she passes the kitchen, she notices his ears are pricked up and he looks intense. Shaking her head, she cleared any bad thoughts from her mind.

She turned on the light on the stairs, climbing wearily up the wooden hill, cleaned her teeth in the bathroom and had a quiet peek into the children's rooms. Seeing them both fast asleep warmed her heart and brought a smile to her face.

It didn't not take her long to get into bed, naked and stretched out the full length of the king size bed. It felt good to lay down and relax, and she sighed, feeling decadent. The room was lit by a little bed-side lamp and the shadows looked larger tonight on the walls. She looked over to the closed curtains over the window and wondered if there was anyone out there, watching the house. Surely Bodie would have barked if there had been, and Ray would have seen them.

She turned onto her side and pulled the sheets up to her chin. Feeling warm and secure in her bed, she found her thoughts drifting to Ray's earlier attitude. She always knew he had his own opinions and would stick by them no matter what, it was something she had always admired about him, but tonight was different. He seemed like another person, someone she did not know. What if he ever lost his temper with her, or even the kids, she wondered, then shook her head. No, he always showed her love and she always felt it from him, she was content here and happy with her man and their life together.

She wondered how long it would be before they came up. Her mind turned to sex, they always had great sex. He was the best she ever had; he could do anything to her and she knew she could do anything to him. Trust from both sides, no inhibitions at all, the thought made her smile. Closing her eyes, she snuggled up under the covers.

She hoped he would not be long and laid there, thinking about the first time they made love, about all the places they had done it, all the times he had made her feel so good, so special. She never opened her eyes again that night, she drifted off and was gone; tiredness and fatigue caught up with her and she fell into a long deep sleep. She didn't know when he came up, she never heard or felt him come to bed.

CHAPTER 9

"Well, I am getting a pony. Ray is going to put some doors on the small barn and I'm keeping her in there," Amber told a half asleep Tommy as she sat on his bed the next morning. She was dressed, washed and ready for the day while he was still half asleep and curled up in his bed.

"Yeah, whatever," he said, disinterested.

"Yes and I am calling her Apple," she said proudly.

"That is a fucking stupid name for a horse."

"Oh, you swore. I'm telling Mum," she said, putting her hand over her mouth even though it was Tommy who said it. She looked shocked and disappointed at the same time at her brother.

"You are not going to get a fucking horse, you stupid idiot. Where are they going to get the money to buy you a horse?"

"You should not be swearing around me."

"Shut up, you stupid idiot." He rolled over and turned away from her.

"You are just jealous anyway," she said, shaking her head at him.

He was turned away from her and she was looking at the back of his head. He said nothing and tried to get back to sleep, she stayed there and just stared at him. After tolerating that for a short while he turned to face her again, saying, "Will you fuck off, you little witch, and leave me alone. I hate this fucking place, I hate being here and I fucking hate you!"

"Well, I hate you too and I hope your head drops off!" She stormed out of the room, her head held high and her nose stuck up in the air. She didn't want to talk to her brother anyway, he was rude and boring most of the time.

She headed downstairs and into the kitchen, then to the back door. She opened this and went outside into the back garden and started to pick some wild flowers that grew there.

She was in her own little world now, humming to herself happyily.

Ray was just waking at this moment, he opened his eyes and saw Diane looking down at him, leaning on one arm and smiling at him as he focused his gaze.

"Good morning, sexy man," she said, smiling.

"Morning, what you doing?" he yawned.

"Watching this sexy fucker who is in my bed."

"Oh, that's okay then. How long have you been looking at me?"

"Oh, about twenty minutes."

"You're fucking mad, do you know that?" he sat up and stretched his arms out, yawning again"

"Takes one to know one" she said with a cheeky smile.

"Well, I'm saying nothing."

"I thought we all could go into town today, take the kids to some civilisation, and besides, we have to go and register with the doctors and the dentist."

"No, I will stay here if you don't mind," he said, looking at her blankly.

"Oh, come on, you have not been away from this place for weeks. You have to get out a bit, it will be fun, and you need to register with the doctors."

"I have a lot to do here still." He slumped back down into the bed.

"But we have to see about a job for you, Ray. Money is running out, love." There was an urgency in her voice which he picked up on instantly.

He frowned at her saying, "I will get a job, don't worry. I just want to make sure this place is right while I have the time on my hands, that's all."

"Nothing needs doing now, well nothing that can't wait anyway. I thought it would be nice for us all to have a day out somewhere, I feel much safer when you're with us anyway."

"I bet that is what the victims of Fred and Rose thought when they got into their car."

"What the hell you on about?" she asked, confused.

"Fred West, he use to drive round with Rose to pick up hitchhikers. The victims thought they were safe with a woman in the car, thought it would be okay to have a lift."

"He was a fucking lunatic." She shook her head.

"I don't know why they had to demolish his house."

"Because who the fuck would live there? I surely wouldn't. And imagine all the freaks that would be going to see the place," she shivered at the thought.

"I would have liked to have seen the place, just to see if there was any feeling or vibrations. You know what I mean, places sometime hold the past, I think."

"Well, your bloody weird. Now are you coming into town or not?"

"Not. I will come with you next time. There are a few things I want to get finished here first, then I will go and find a job, okay?" He smiled at her, then winked.

"Oh, you are bloody useless when you are like this." She got off the bed and went to the bathroom; Ray just pulled the covers over his shoulders and turned over for a few more minutes of sleep.

After she had washed, she woke her son, then went downstairs and talked to her daughter about what she wanted for breakfast. When Tommy came down a short time later they all had cornflakes at the table and were discussing where to go that day.

"I want to go to the cinema," Tommy piped up.

"Yeah, so do I. What is showing?" Amber asked.

"We will see when we get into town. I want you both to ring your dad today as well."

"Okay. Is Ray coming with us?" Amber asked.

"No not today, he has some work to do on the house."

"When is he going to fix the barn so I can get my pony?"

"Oh shut up about that horse, Amber," Tommy complained.

"Don't start, either of you," Diane told them firmly, pointing her finger at them in turn. "Ray says you should not point your finger, because you have three fingers on the same hand pointing back at you," Amber says to no one in particular as she eat her cereal. Tommy looked confused and pointed his finger in the air, trying to make out what she meant, finally realising then smiling to himself.

"We are going to get you two registered with the doctor and the dentist, so I don't want any argument if you have to have an appointment to see them at any time." Both children nodded their heads at their mother, but did not look too convincing.

After breakfast they got ready to go into town. Ray looked fast asleep when Diane went up to tell him they were going, so she gently kissed him on the cheek and left very quietly so as not to awaken him. She need not have bothered, though, for as soon as the front door was closed, Ray opened his eyes. He waited until he heard his car pull out of the gates, then jumped out of bed and was dressed in a matter of moments.

He went down to the kitchen and greeted Bodie, both of them fussing over each other for a few minutes, then he let his faithful dog out the back door. Walking over to the stairs, he opened the wooden door on the side and leaned in under the stairs, moving some boxes, then a suitcase, until he found what he was looking for.

He lifted the taped cardboard box out and took it into the front room. Pulling at the tape on one corner, he ripped it off the top of the box and began looking inside. Moving some things around as he searched the contents, he came across a phone charger and then a small mobile, the children's, but he ignored them, throwing them back into the box. They were not what he was looking for, so he dug deeper into the box, finally finding what he sought.

The planchette, which he pulled out and put it on the floor by his side. He searched again, and it didn't take him long to find the board, which he lifted free of the box, pushing the box away. He placed the board on the floor and opened it. It was an old ouija board that looked worn and well used, yellow in colour with a row of numbers at the top and the alphabet in a circle round the edge. At the bottom of the board there was a simple 'yes' or 'no' option. Plain but effective.

He had tried, on many occasions, to discover if his dream, the one he'd been having since he was a child, was important. And, as usually happened, he never received a reply that he understood.

"Yes" was always the answer to the question of whether or not he was a warrior, though he'd never really hurt anyone in his life.

Putting that aside, he placed the planchette on to the surface and smiled, putting both his hands on the pointer and closing his eyes.

CHAPTER 10

Diane had good day out with her children, they all enjoyed themselves and had got done what they wanted to do. They were in a jubilant mood, happily smiling and laughing. Amber was wearing a bright yellow top that she had found in a sale, as it was only a matter of a few pounds, Diane bought it for her. She was so pleased and proud of her new top and couldn't wait to show Ray.

As they came up the hill, they had to slow and stop for some riders on horseback. Amber stared with her mouth hanging open at the large animals as they strode past their car. Diane pulled to one side to let them pass. When she had begun to drive on, Amber looked out the back window at the riders until they turned and were gone.

Reaching the gates, the car was pulled in slowly to the yard and up to the front of the house. Ray was standing at the door watching Bodie rummaging around and he did not take much notice of the car at first, but finally turned and walked to it when the children got out.

Diane went to the boot and took some bags of shopping out and walked to the front door, looking at Ray, who was unshaven and rough-looking. "Bloody hell, have you been in a fight?" she asked jokingly.

"Why you say that?"

"You look rough, dear," she said as she reached him and gave him a kiss. He looked at the bags and then at Amber as she came up to him and did a spin to show off her new top. "Doesn't she look sexy in her new top?" Diane asked.

"It was only a few pounds, Ray, cheap at half the price. Do you like it?" She was grinning from ear to ear, her joy was unmistakable.

"Well, you do know if you go out in the sun in a bright yellow top like that, it will be covered in fly shit by the end of the day."

"No, I won't," Amber said, dejected, her face falling into a sad expression.

"You will. Yellow attracts flies, they will think you're a big flower and shit on you."

"Don't tell her that," she said to Ray. Turning to Amber she said, "You ignore him, love, you look beautiful." She went into the house past Ray, looking at him questioningly as she did, followed by Tommy, and then Amber. He waited for a moment, then whistled for Bodie, who came running over and followed Ray back into the house.

"I have been in touch with the telephone people today," he said as he shut the door.

"Oh yeah, what did they say?" asked Diane enthusiastically from the kitchen. Ray walked in and sat down by the table before answering her.

"Are you ready?" he asked with baited breath.

"Go on," she said turning to face him, leaning back against the kitchen sink.

"They said because there is no line to the house, they will have to come and connect one and, because we're so far away from the beaten path and telegraph pole, it will be a difficult job."

"And?" she waited for the answer she knew she was not going to want to hear.

"We're talking around four hundred pounds."

"Oh fuck off, that is bloody ridiculous!" She shook her head in disbelief.

"And the good news is, it might take up to five weeks before they can come and do it."

"Well they can go and fuck themselves, I am buying some cheap mobiles when I go into town again. There is no way I am paying that much for a bloody bit of wire to my house."

Ray stood and went up to her, he put his arms round her and gave her a welcoming hug. She hugged him back and they held each other for a few moments.

"Did you have a good day, anyway?" Ray asked her finally.

"Yes we did. I have to take them back next week for an appointment with the doctor and dentist, so I will get some cheap phones then. They're only about twenty quid each for a basic one, that will have to do for now. I wonder where the charger and phone went, I just can't see us losing them."

"Well, we searched all the boxes didn't we?" Ray said, smiling at her.

"Oh, I'm sorry babe, I didn't mean to take it out on you, it has just pissed me off, that's all."

"Look, you go and get a shower or a nice bath and I will make you a cuppa." He smiled at her and she smiled back, then nodded her head and went upstairs, leaving him to make the tea in the kitchen. As he was doing so, Amber walked in and sat down, looking at him.

"You alright, Ray?" she asked politely.

"Yeah mate, I'm not too bad for a young en," he said, smiling.

"But you're not young," she replied.

"Amber, why is a nymphomaniac like a doorknob?"

"I do not know what a nymphomaniac is," she said naively.

Ignoring her statement, he replied, "Every one gets a turn."

"I just do not get your jokes, Ray, they are very silly."

He came over and sat next to her at the table, she smiled and he smiled back, asking, "Where is your brother?"

"Upstairs on his play station. He said he wants a bigger TV for it, the portable he has is too small," she mocked, rolling her eyes and shaking her head.

"Oh well, bully for him. What a dilemma." Ray shook his head in disgust.

"I know, he should be grateful for what he has got," she said, sounding very adult for a moment.

"Yes, Amber, you are right. You both should be very grateful for what you have."

"Yes, I am very happy with my new top. You do like it, don't you?" She looked at him then at the bright yellow top she was wearing.

"Yes, Amber, it is lovely. Just don't go out in the sun wearing it," he grinned at her.

"I don't care if flies come near me anyway," she boasted.

"Two flies walked up a mirror, and one said to the other, 'Well, that's one way of looking at it.'" He smiled at her and waited then waited a moment for her reaction.

"Is that a joke, Ray?" she asked with a frown and a confused look on her face, as she looked over the rim of her glasses like a schoolteacher questioning one of her students.

"If you cross a chiropodist and a psychopath, do you get a foot path?"

"What is a chiropodist, Ray" she asked.

"Amber, listen, who said, 'We will fight them on the beaches'?"

"I don't know."

"Winston Churchill."

"Oh yeah, the prime minister when the war was on with Germany," she said proudly, remembering the conversation they had about it the other day.

"Yes, very good, but who said, 'Defeat is bad'?"

"I don't know," she shook her head with a baffled look on her face.

"Nelson Mandela's chiropodist," Ray said smiling, stopping when he saw Amber looking at him blankly.

"You don't like jokes much, do you Amber?" he asked her.

"Yes I do, when they are funny," she smiled.

"Okay then, you tell me a funny joke." He looked at her and waited while she thought, cocking her head to one side and looking up into space for a moment while she tried to come up with a joke. He waited patiently, watching as she whispered to herself then stopped, shaking her head, thinking very hard.

Eventually she gave up and let out a long breath, as if what she had just done a very tiring thing. "I can't think of one," she told him.

"Ok, what goes in cold, comes out wet and the longer it stands, the stronger it gets?"

"I don't know," she said quickly.

"Well, have a think while I make a cup of tea. Do you want one?"

"Yes, please," she said, still trying to answer the riddle. Ray stood and made the tea and it was not long before Diane came back down. Her hair was wet and she was in jogging bottoms and a loose tee shirt.

Walking in, she took a mug of tea from the counter and looked at Ray and Amber sitting at the table, saying, "What have you two been talking about then?"

"Nothing much. Amber is just working out a riddle," Ray told her.

"Mum, what goes in dry, comes out wet and the longer it stands, the stronger it gets?" Amber asked her while taking a sip of her tea.

"What are you drinking, love?" Diane asked with a little smile on her face.

"A cup of tea," she replied, not understanding the point.

"Yeah, think about it, isn't tea dry when you put it into the pot? Then wet when you pour it out, and if you leave it to stand, doesn't it go strong?"

"Oh yeah," she smiled and laughed, looking at Ray.

"Well done," Diane said.

"Give me another one, Ray, another riddle."

"What goes in dry and hard, but comes out wet and soft?" He looked up at Diane who was wide-eyed, looking back at him in disbelief. Amber went straight into deep thought, thinking very hard. She looked at her mum, who just gave a slight smile, unsure of the answer that Ray was going to give her young, innocent daughter. Amber looked at Ray, confused but trying to think of an answer, eventually shaking her head at him.

"Do you want me to give you the answer?"

"Yes," she said eagerly.

"Are we sure we want to hear it?" Diane questioned dubiously.

"Chewing gum," Ray announced, grinning at Diane.

"Chewing gum?" Amber asked.

"Think about it," Ray told her.

"Oh right, yeah, I see. That's good Ray, I'm going to tell Tommy that one. Did you know that one Mum?" She looked up at her mother and was confused as to why she was shaking her head at Ray and smiling.

"Yes love, very good," she said looking down at her while holding her laugh at bay. It sounded so strange for her young daughter to be saying this, knowing that her own answer to the riddle was completely different to what Amber thought.

"Well, if you two don't mind, I think I will go and watch some telly." She took her drink and left the kitchen while Diane took the chair that she'd just abandoned. She looked at Ray and grinned.

"What?" he asked innocently.

"You fucking know what," she said, smiling.

"I've no idea what you're on about. The answer was chewing gum, what else could it be?"

"Of course it is, dear."

"Your face was a picture, mind," he said, chuckling.

"You have to be careful what you say, they will be going into school and telling their mates this stuff, you know."

"Well it will make them very popular, if you ask me. Do you feel better after your shower?" he asked, casually changing the subject.

"Oh yeah, much better. It was nice and refreshing. Shall we have an early night tonight, that is if there is nothing about psychos or weirdoes, or mass-murdering maniacs on

the telly that you want to watch," she said jokingly.

"Well come to mention it… No there isn't" he smiled.

CHAPTER 11

The rain started about three hours later, a steady rain, though not a hard downpour. The house was all locked up, they were all in for the night. Only one light was on, the one in the main room where Ray and Diane were sitting. Outside it had become dull and wet, the night sky was dropping in and the cold could be felt in the air.

How he got there was only known to him, but he had, and he had done it quietly, stealthily. Perched on the roof next to the chimney stack was the gaunt, fragile thing that lived in the small barn. Crouched down next to the brick stack for shelter from the rain, he looked out across to the lake.

The rain was dripping from his head and he was soaked to the skin, but it did not seem to bother him. He stared into the distance, across to the stretch of water beyond while raindrops that had trickled down from his forehead dropped from the end of his nose.

Breathing heavily, he sat with one of his hands on his hammer, which was down his belt, and the other resting across his knee, which was raised. He resembled a sentinel, but what he was looking for only he knew.

Many a night he had sat here, always unnoticed. He was quite unhappy about the residents in the house and the dog they had brought with them. He hated dogs and felt that he had to keep away from them. The daytime was the hardest time for him.

He sniffed, his nose up in the air, then shivered. He was motionless for a few more minutes then arose from his crouched position. He stretched out and moved his gaze over to the woods; he had a good view from up here and could see all the surrounding area, very well.

It was another half hour before he moved again. Slowly and silently he made his way to the end of the roof. He eased his light, little body over the side, then carefully climbed down the side wall with great skill. He knew all the little holes his hands could fit in and the little ledges for his feet; to anyone else, the wall would have seemed impossible to climb or descend, but he did and was running towards the woods when Bodie let out a bark from within the house. He was gone down the road, trotting at a steady pace, gaining speed as he reached the end of the tree line. He soon leapt into the wooded area and seemed, to the human eye, to just vanish.

The rain was falling steadily, wetting all it touched, and the night air became damp. Sitting with his mouth open, the fragile figure was on the floor of the forest, although the trees did not offer much shelter. He looked set in stone, not moving, not even blinking that much; silent, motionless, and soaked to his skin through the old rags he was wearing.

Licking his lips to get the last drop of water off them, he moved and looked round. He was struggling to find food this night, crawling on the ground he went to a fallen tree branch. He looked around as if to check the coast was clear, then he lifted the branch up, exposing the damp soil beneath. Throwing the branch off to one side, he reached down and took the long worm that was making its way back underground after being disturbed. He ate this in one go, only chewing a few times before swallowing. He proceeded to pick at the insects and beetles that were living there, eating anything that moved without seeming to taste it.

When he had cleared the patch, he stood and walked away deeper into the trees, wiping the dirt and mud off his mouth with the back of his hand. His bare feet were tough and rough, having been hardened over time, and he walked steadily over any terrain without trouble. Every now and then he flicked his head to one side when he heard something, staying motionless for a few moments, looking, checking , then carrying on his way, always searching for food.

Several hours later, he was creeping back across the side of the house, moving carefully and quietly. He came to the black bin liner that was next to the dustbin; he had found food here before and hoped to again. He tore at the black bag, ripping it open. Crouching down and picking through the scraps of food that were inside, some old potato peels, leftover meal scraped from a plate, anything he could eat he did. Discarding the bag, with its contents scattered across the ground, he made his way back to the small barn. The rain had stopped but the air was still damp and moist.

He was cold and wanted to get dry, so he went into the barn and scrambled up a beam and the side of the wooden wall to his dry place of rest. Taking his hammer out of his belt, he put it carefully and softly next to him, as if it was a living being and he didn't want to harm it. Settling down, he curled up on the straw and old sack that he slept on. Shivering and staring, he finally fell motionless, quiet and statue-like.

It had not been a good night for him. He was finding it more and more difficult to find food with the occupants in the house, and finding it more and more difficult to avoid them. It was becoming much more difficult to survive. His eyes eventually closed and that's where the pathetic figure remained until he was ready to go hunting for food once more.

CHAPTER 12

"Is he okay?" Diane asked as Ray came back into the bedroom.

"Yeah, he is settled again. He will soon get used to the place, don't worry."

"Come on, get back into bed then, you sexy sod." She smiled coyly at him and lifted the covers for him to crawl back under. He was wearing only his boxer shorts and she admired him as he slid into the bed next to her. He smiled at the warmth and welcoming pleasure the bed offered and opened his arms wide for her to cuddle into his side. There they lay, comfortably snuggled together.

"We saw some horses today on the road as we came up," Diane said to him.

"Bloody horses, they're a right pain on the road."

"Don't say that to Amber, she loves horses."

"Yeah, but why the hell should they be allowed on the road?"

"Well, how the hell are they going to get from place to place?" she questioned.

"No, I don't believe in it. They are a bloody pain, and dangerous besides. Sometimes the riders are only kids, what happens when that horse bolts? There's no way a child will stop it, not even an adult for that matter. And what about the fucking shit they never clean up? If your dog craps on the road you get fined, but a horse craps all over the fucking place and they just leave it. It pisses me off."

"Don't start getting worked up again, I only mentioned we saw some horses," she said to him.

"No, listen, if a farmer leaves mud on the road, he has to clean it up, by law, because of cars skidding and stuff. So why not a fucking horse? Bloody horse shit would be lethal to a motorbike that came around a corner and hit it, you would be right off. And, if they bolt and wreck your fucked. Do they have insurance?" he asked her, frowning.

"I imagine so, yes"

"I will bet that most don't bother. Anyway, they hold traffic up, most of them refuse to ride single file. They piss me right off! Fucking horse should be in a field and, if they have to be moved, then they should be put in a horse box, not rode on the highway where there are cars. It is dangerous and fucking stupid, if you ask me." He leaned back on the pillow and put both his hands behind his head, looking at the ceiling.

"Is there anything you don't complain about?" Diane asked him, not completely serious, but not totally joking.

"Yes, lots of things," he smiled and turned his head to look at her.

"Oh, that's good then," she smiled back at him.

"Every man should be entitled to his own opinion." he told her.

"Yes they should, and there is an argument for every opinion, don't you think?"

"Arguments are sometimes counter-productive."

"Which means you're always right?"

"No, not at all, but I'm not always wrong. It's just that the truth scares a lot of people," he said, his smile fading.

"I must agree there, it sometimes does. Now smile again. You look so bloody sexy when you smile," she grinned at him, running her hand across his chest suggestively. It took some time, but eventually they fell asleep.

***

Ray was up and ready early the next morning. He had left Diane asleep in bed, she wanted a lie in. He was drinking a glass of milk in the kitchen, Amber was in her night dress sitting at the table and Tommy was up early for a change, also, sitting with a bowl of cereal in front of him. Ray took a banana from the fruit bowl, he looking at Amber and asking, "Hey Amber, count the skins for me."

"What do you mean?" she asked, looking at him. Tommy looked up as well.

"Watch," Ray said as he peeled a skin off the banana. "That's one skin."

"One skin," Amber said, watching as he peeled another. She then said, "Two skin." He repeated his action and she said, "Three skin." Looking at Tommy with a twinkle in his eye, he peeled one last time and Amber said, "Four skin."

Tommy dropped his spoon and started to laugh uncontrollably; his head was rocking and he leaned forward holding his mouth, unable to stop himself.

Amber became annoyed and shouted at him. "What are you laughing at? I got it right, it was four skin." She looked at Ray for support, but he just smiled and ate the banana, so she turned back to Tommy, hitting him across the table. He moved out of the way and laughed at her, then he looked at Ray and nodded his head in agreement. He liked that joke and found it most amusing.

Ray left them there, Tommy was having a good laugh and Amber was becoming more annoyed with him because she didn't understand what he was laughing at. "Bodie, come here" Ray commanded to his dog. They both went out of the front door, closing it behind them. Ray took a big lung full of the crisp clear air while Bodie stretched his legs and body.

Looking around, Ray noticed it straight away from where he was standing. He walked over and looked down, staring at a small foot print left in the mud. Looking around in no particular direction he stood on it and covered it with his own foot print, the boots he had on disguised it perfectly.

Minutes later they were both walking down the small road towards the woods. Bodie was trotting ahead and Ray was enjoying the time he had alone with his dog. He loved this time when he could just go out and no one was around, just him and Bodie. They cut off the road and into the woods, which was damp and fresh smelling after the rain. Bodie did his usual scouting and searching while Ray walked behind him, watching his companion with glee.

They went deeper into the woods than they had been before and, after about fifteen minutes, Bodie stopped, looking confused. He turned and watched his master walking towards him and, although this seemed to make him feel better, he was still troubled by something.

It was something that could not be seen, but he could sense it, and it was a strong feeling. He walked back to Ray, who reassured him with a pat on the head and a rub of his back, and they carried on. Bodie, however, stayed closer to Ray than he had done when they first set out; he was in more 'guard' mode than 'explore' mode all of a sudden.

Ray's boots were getting muddy and Bodie's paws were the same, but it did not seem to bother either of them. The trees seemed to be more alive after the rain, looking as if they were trying to escape from the ground and reach up to the sky in contorted shapes.

It was sunny today, but the forest had held much of the damp air in, it still seemed sticky and clammy, the humidity had been held over from the storm. No one was about, none of that noise of everyday living, and the feeling of solitude was growing stronger all the time.

Ray liked it here, it was what he felt at home with, his own company. He walked looking straight ahead until he heard a bird fly past his head above. He looked up and tried to spot it, he turned and walked backwards, trying to follow the bird with his eyes.

Because he wasn't looking, he did not see it, did not see where the ground was a different colour, where it had been eroded by the rain. He did not see the hole that had appeared and he stepped straight into it, his weight taking him down and back.

Bodie barked and ran closer, he saw his master disappear from his sight, down into a muddy ditch of a hole. Running to the lip he looked down, barking into it; he could see his master lying still at the bottom of the muddy, grave-like hole.

Ray stirred and sat up, his ears ringing and his head sore where he had hit it on the side of the hole as he fell. He looked up and smiled at his dog, who peering down at him, lifting his arm to reassure him. Bodie's tail began to wag and his bark changed, now he barked not so much with fear and urgency, but with happy relief. He yapped for a few moments then sat, watching Ray as he stood and shook himself off. He moved slowly, assessing the damage. The fall had not been too bad, and the soft earth had helped to break the impact.

Looking up, he could see that the deep hole was purposely dug, but what for he did not know. He reached up as far as he could, but his hand was still about four feet from the top. Bits of soil were still falling in on him from the edge and sides. It was then he noticed the foul smell that seemed to emanate from the walls of this open tomb. He curled up his nostrils and kicked the side of the muddy wall, trying to make a foot hold about two feet from the bottom.

The soil was harder in the wall but he still managed to kick a decent hole, large enough to get his foot into. He then slipped his foot into the hole and reached out, spanning his arms across the chamber's width, and lifted his body weight up. He placed his other foot on the opposite wall, kicking it in as he did; he now stood about two feet higher than he had been before.

Holding his body weight mostly on the foot he had dug into the muddy wall, he kicked with his other foot to do the same on the opposite side, to give himself another leverage point. He thumped the wall with his right fist just above his head and then grabbed fistfuls of dirt to get a handhold into the soil. He was making good progress, another couple of these and he should be out, he thought.

Bodie stood as he saw him getting higher; he wanted to help but could do nothing except watch with anticipation and eagerness.

Ray flinched as he grabbed a handful of soil out of the hole he had just punched into the side of the wall. A pain ran through his hand, he retracted it quickly; his reflex fast, spontaneous. He looked at his hand and saw that it had been sliced, a sharp implement of some kind had cut in from his little finger to his wrist. He looked up, trying to see what had cut him, but the hole was a bit too high for him to see into.

He decided to carry on and deal with his hand later, he wanted out of this big hole as quickly as he had fallen into it. He carefully put his wounded hand back into the hole, gently feeling for a safe grip. Pulling his weight up once again, he kicked a foot hole into the opposite wall, spreading out and stretching across the hole to get a fixed point so that he could rest. He then put his other foot on a welcome root of a tree that was sticking out as if to aide him in his climb. He turned and looked into the hand hole to see what had cut him, backing off slightly when he saw the soil fall away to reveal what was behind it, what had carved into his hand.

It was the open mouth of a dead dog. He must have punched into the open jaws and the bottom teeth had ripped his hand open. Its eyes were open and it was on its side, buried, the jaw was hanging open and blood was just visible on the bottom teeth. Ray's blood. He looked at it for a few moments, then looked round his enclosure. Looking carefully, he could just make out the back leg of a dog on the opposite wall, barely visible through the wet soil.

Looking up, he could see that he was almost out, though the walls were damper up here and were not as solid. He still had about another foot to go before he could reach out of the pit and hopefully pull himself free. Reaching as far as he could, he pulled at the soil for another hand hole to work his way up.

He lifted his leg and again kicked at the side of the muddy wall, but instead of a hole developing as before, a large section of the soil gave way and dropped to the bottom of the hole. With the soil fell the remains of two dogs, formerly very large and powerful, but limp now, dropping like a sack of heavy potatoes to the bottom of the pit.

They were lifeless, but somehow very disturbing. They did not seem totally dead. It unnerved Bodie and he whimpered, then gave a nervous bark. Ray looked down at them and knew something was very wrong, he just did not know what it was, something did not look right or feel right.

Kicking again, he made a hole for his foot this time and he scrambled up, throwing his body up as high as he could, he pushed and reached until he was able to finally reach the top and hold on. His legs were still dangling into the hole but most of his upper body was out and he snatched at the ground to heave himself free. Bodie, standing in front of him, instinctively grabbed his sleeve in his mouth and pulled backwards. The full power of this large brute of a dog pulled his master up and free of the pit.

Ray could hear the walls give way and collapse just as he was free. He lay there on his back panting while Bodie came to him and licked his face with joy and relief, his tail wagging like a propeller. "If it goes any faster," Ray thought, "he will take off." Still breathing heavily, Ray stroked his dog, then rolled over and stood up. He initially backed away from the hole, but then slowly and carefully he walked to the edge, looking into the dark pit. He could see nothing now that the soil had collapsed back into it from the top and sides.

He knelt down and fussed over Bodie, thanking him for his help. They were both very happy he was out of the hole and it showed in their faces and actions towards each other. Taking his handkerchief from his pocket, he wrapped it around his hand and backed off, turning to head back to the house.

He was covered in mud and dirt, his shirt was ripped and his jeans were torn at the knees, not that he was concerned with what he looked like. What did concern him was the sight of dead dogs. He did not like to even think about how they got there, just the idea disturbed him. But, looking down at his ever faithful dog, Bodie, as he trotted alongside him, calmed him and he smiled slightly.

The rest of the way home, he thought what to tell Diane, but before he got there he stopped suddenly and sat on a fallen tree. He sighed and looked up, then buried his head in

his hands, resting his elbows on his knees. Bodie laid next to him, not taking his eyes off him

for a moment. It was an hour before Ray moved from this spot, he got lost in his own

thoughts as he tried to get his head straight and his nerves calm again. Finally he stood,

stretched, and then walked the rest of the way home.

Out of the woods and onto the small road, they headed up the hill towards their home.

Bodie was walking right next to Ray, refusing to leave him for a moment since he'd dragged

his master out of the hole. He sensed that something was wrong and knew he had to stick to

his master at all costs; he had known something was not right in the woods from his first

explorations, but he could do nothing about it. He felt it more strongly than Ray did, the

uneasy, unsettling atmosphere that surrounded the woods, and the scent of death and suffering

he picked up when he sniffed the ground.

They both walked briskly and it didn't take them long to reach the gates. Stopping to

gather his nerve, Ray looked down at his companion and smiled a reassuring smile, more for

himself than his dog, and then carried on up to the house. They went in, Ray taking off his

boots as he went through the door.

"Diane" he shouted, but no reply came. Bodie went to his water bowl and lapped up a

good long drink, Ray, following him into into the kitchen, saw a note on the table.

"Took kids to the lake for a walk round. Won't be long. Love, Diane." She had put

five X's at the end, which made him smile. Taking his opportunity, he went upstairs and got a

shower and changed his clothes. He cleaned up his hand the best that he could then put the

clothes into the wash basket and cleaned up where he had made a mess with his muddy attire

and bloody hand.

Finishing that job, he walked back through the kitchen and out the door. Walking the

short distance to the lake he soon saw Diane and her children, throwing stones into the water.

He approached with Bodie, as ever, by his side.

They were standing on the water's edge, looking across the lake. Diane turned nervously when she heard something behind her, smiling when she saw that it was Ray. She looked down and noticed the large plaster on his hand, instantly concerned. "Oh, what have you done?" she asked.

"Just had a fall in the woods, made a muddy mess of my clothes and cut my hand. Nothing to worry about," he said, shrugging. He smiled and pulled the hand away from her, putting it around her shoulder and she looked down at Bodie who was sitting, as if on guard duty, next to Ray.

"You alright?" she asked, looking back at Ray.

"Yeah, I'm fine. Are you? Did you have a good lay in this morning?"

"Not much, but I am refreshed," she smiled at him and held onto him in a loving way, with her arms round his waist.

"That's good," he said, looking out across the lake.

"Are you okay, love? You seem a bit distant," Diane said, worried.

"I'm fine, no problem," he said, smiling down at her and giving her a squeeze. They both watched the children playing by the lake, throwing in stones and trying to make them skim across the water.

"They wanted to go swimming," Diane said, still watching her kids play.

"I don't think that is a good idea. You should keep them out of the water" Ray stated.

"I think they will be okay when the weather gets warmer. They are both good swimmers." She looked up at him.

"No, I don't think you should let them swim in the lake. It is too dangerous," he said, staring intently into the distance.

"They will be fine so long as they don't go too far out. They could get a big inflatable rubber ring and some stuff like that."

"Keep them out of the bloody water," Ray shouted, looking down at her with an angry frown on his face.

"What's up with you?" she demanded, standing back from him. Just as suddenly as it appeared, the fierce expression changed and he apologised, taking hold of her and pulling her back to him.

"I'm sorry didn't mean to shout, but water scares the hell out of me. I can't swim. Anyway, we took millions of years to get out of the sea and I don't think we should go back there."

"It's not the bloody sea, it's a lake, and the kids love to swim. I suppose, though, it's nice that you have some concern. Why can't you swim?"

"My cock is too big and it keeps pulling me down to the bottom," he said, smiling at her cheekily.

She play punched him and laughed, then they both walked down the short distance to where the children were playing and stood watching them with their arms around one another. "It's lovely here, Ray," Diane said, looking out across the water and beyond with a contented expression on her face.

"Yes it is, very lovely," Ray agreed. He looked over his shoulder to where Bodie was watching, guarding his master. Looking back across the water, Ray held Diane a little tighter and a little closer to him, she felt so warm and loving to him. He slowly clenched his fist as the cut on his hand began to throb, then released it again.

He had cleaned the wound with antiseptic and stopped it bleeding, but it was now throbbing and he moved his fingers to get the feeling back into them. The healing process had begun and now had to run its course. He was thinking of the sight of the dogs in the hole, wondering why they didn't seem as decomposed as they should. He couldn't understand how they looked so fresh? Just how long had they been there.

He shook the thought from his mind for now and tried not to think of it again that day.

CHAPTER 13

Every mother knows the real fear in the scream of their child, and Diane was awoke with such a noise, a screaming of absolute terror, unbalanced fear, and petrified helplessness. She dashed from the bedroom, leaving Ray to awaken more slowly.

She ran into Amber's room and turned on the light, seeing her daughter sitting up in bed, sweating profusely and clutching the bed sheets to chest. She looked over to her mother with a start when she ran in, then held her arms out as she was shaking and crying, near hysterics.

"What is it, baby?" Diane asked, concerned, running to her daughter and holding her in her arms as she sat on her bed. Amber held to her mother tightly, as if her life depended on it. She was crying so hard that she could not speak at first, gasping as she tried to catch her breath.

Diane lifted her up and took her to her room, Ray was out of bed and on his way, stopping when Diane entered again. She sat on the bed, and put Amber on her knee, rocking her gently and stroking her head, trying to calm and comfort her. Tommy appeared at the bedroom door rubbing his eyes, still half asleep.

"What is it, Mum? What's wrong?" he asked.

"Nothing, go back to bed, love. Amber just had a bad dream," Diane told him kindly but firmly. He glanced at Amber then his mother, and finally up at Ray, who was looking down at him. He said nothing and went slowly back to his room, closing the door behind him.

"What is it, sweetheart, what's wrong?" Diane asked her daughter.

"People, horrid people, Mummy," she managed to say, unable to continue. She held her mother tight, sobbing into her breast and making a wet patch on her night dress.

"It was a bad dream, baby, that's all. You're safe, don't worry."

"What people?" Ray asked, walking up to Diane and kneeling down to come to

Amber's eye level.

"Scary, ugly, horrid people," she said to him, crying and shaking.

"Where, Amber, where did you see them? In your room?" He stared intently as he waited for her reply.

"No, I was in the kitchen. There were people hanging up from the walls and red blood everywhere," she sobbed, holding her mother just that much tighter.

"Did you go downstairs, baby?" Diane asked her as Ray left the room and walked down into the kitchen.

"I awoke and I was in my bed, Mummy," she cried.

"Darling, it was just a dream, that's all. You had a nightmare, it's not real, sweetheart."

"It was horrible, Mummy, ugly people cutting up bodies, and all that blood," her voice faltered and Diane pulled her close to her, giving her comfort and love.

"Shhh, now, come on, you are safe. I won't let anyone hurt you, and no one will ever hurt you while I am around, I promise you that. You have just had a very bad dream, it's not real."

Amber pulled back and seemed to calm a little, she looked into her mother's eyes and smiled slightly. Her breathing had steadied and she was returning back to her normal self.

Ray came back in, looking at them both in turn as he walked to the bed. "Nothing down there, no one, nothing," he smiled reassuringly at Amber.

"See. Anyway, Bodie would have seen them off." Diane patted her daughter's knee comfortingly.

"He would that," Ray said to her, grinning.

Amber took a big sigh and dried her eyes with the back of her hand, sniffling. Diane took her to the bathroom to clean her up and Ray could hear her reassuring her daughter all the way down to the landing and into the bathroom.

He got back into bed and laid there for several minutes, then heard them come out of the bath room and go back into Amber's room. It was another twenty minutes before Diane came back. "Is she okay?" he asked.

"Rocked her back to sleep, poor love," she said, getting back into bed.

"Something scared her there?" Ray enquired rather than stated.

"She has not had nightmares for years, bless her."

"What did she say she saw in the kitchen?"

"Oh I don't know, it's a child's mind, bit graphic though."

"Dead bodies, wasn't it? Hung up in the kitchen?"

"Something like that. I mean, where the hell did she get that from, was it something that she saw on the television? What could have brought that on?" She looked at him quizzically.

"Don't know," he replied, shrugging. "Young children see things that we can't, I think. They are more receptive to their surroundings, more vulnerable to the energy around us all."

"What the bloody hell are you on about?" Diane looked at him, confused and a little concerned.

"Dead bodies hung up in the kitchen?"

"Ray, you are bloody scaring me now. My daughter has just had probably the worst experience of her life and you are not making sense to me."

"I just think children are more in touch with their surroundings then we are. They have imaginary friends don't they? People say, 'oh, it's just a passing thing', but how do we know they don't really have someone there that they are communicating with?"

"Oh shut up! She had a bloody nightmare, that's all," Diane said, sounding agitated.

"But a very vivid nightmare about dead bodies cut up in the kitchen, decapitated and hung on the walls, blood all over the place, ugly family doing it?"

"Ugly family? She never said that." Diane sat up and looked at him, frowning. She was a little confused and seemed to be thinking to herself for a moment before turning back to look at him.

"She said ugly people, didn't she?" Ray said, defending himself.

"Yeah. Is there something you're not telling me, Ray?" she demanded.

"What do you mean?"

"I don't know, it is just strange that you are so interested. Normally you just leave the kids to me, but now you are all questions and fascinated. Why is that?"

"I am just taking an interest, I do have to learn about these things. I told you before that I am alien with kids and have to learn all I can. If I had been here by myself when that happened, I would not of been sure what to do. I don't have the mother's instinct like you."

"You don't need it to calm a child after a nightmare, you're not that stupid. You know that all she needs is a comforting hug and calming words. You could have done that, I'm sure."

"Well I will know in future, won't I? Why are you getting all angry with me?"

"I don't know, sorry. I'm probably a little upset about Amber, that's all." She laid back down and looked up at the ceiling, while Ray laid flat and did the same. There was silence for a moment, until Ray broke it.

"You alright? Have I upset you?" he asked, concerned.

"I'm fine. You're not holding back anything on me, are you?"

"What like? What do you mean?"

"I don't know, it is just strange to me that you are so interested in this. Normally you just don't bother, if it had been a nightmare about big purple spiders or something, you would have just dismissed it, but because it is gruesome and horrible, you are all ears and want to drill my daughter about it. Why is that?" Her voice was solid and cold and Ray didn't like it. He turned and faced her.

"I'm sorry, I didn't mean to upset you. It's just my morbid fascination, I suppose, the way I am. We all have an interest."

"You haven't been letting her watch your bloody stupid programs about murders and killers and such, have you?" She turned her head and looked at him, her eyes cold and her face expressionless. "Can you keep your interest away from my kids in future, please?"

"I have not shown her anything or told her anything. This is not my bloody fault!"

"She must have gotten that image from somewhere, Ray. Someone must have put it in her head. A ten year old child does not have these images in her mind by herself."

"Now just fucking wait a minute," he began, but before he could say any more, Diane got off the bed.

Turning to face him, she glared at him. "I don't like being swore at. I am going to sleep with Amber tonight, in case she wakes up again. I will see you in the morning." She turned to go and stopped, remembering something.

"I suggest you go into town and start looking for a job, Ray. The money is almost gone and we are going to start to struggle big time soon."

Before he could answer, she was gone, the door closed behind her. He contemplated going after her for a moment, but thought against it as soon as it entered his head. He lay back on the bed and, as he put his hands behind his head, he flinched a little as he caught his cut on the pillow.

Diane had never walked out of the room like that on him before. He was alone again with his thoughts and he had to make so many decisions. He knew that he had to try to find a job, she was right, as she usually was.

He finally closed his eyes and drifted off to sleep, only awaken again an hour later. Feeling uneasy he got out of bed to go to the bathroom. As he walked down the stairs, he noticed that the kitchen light was on, finding Diane at the table with a mug of half drunk coffee in her hand when he entered. She was silent, staring into the mug like a fortune teller.

He slowly walked over and sat down across the table from her. They said nothing for a moment until he decided to break the silence. "Are you okay? What is wrong?" His voice was caring and concerned.

"I'm alright" she said quietly, but unconvincingly, as she took a drink of her coffee. She still did not look at him.

"I'm sorry if I have upset you."

"It's alright. I suppose I'd better get used to it." She finally looked at him with tears in her eyes.

"I don't mean to hurt you and I am sorry if I have. It was unintentional."

"I'm scared, Ray, scared it will all go wrong."

He reached out and took her hand. Holding it, he looked her in the eye and said quietly, "It is going to be fine, babe."

"I hope so. I get this feeling that something is wrong, that you don't really like my kids. You seem different since we've been here, more reclusive. I don't know. Before when you used to stay with us or we stayed with you, you interacted with them, played with them and things. It all just seems different now since we have been living together under the same roof." Her voice was full of hurt and confusion.

"It is not like that. You know I get on with the kids, look at all the jokes I tell Amber." He smiled and she did too, just a little.

"Yeah, but you don't always seem happy with them. Are you regretting what we have done?"

"Diane, we have already been through all this."

"Is this not what you expected?" She started to sob and tears dripped from he eyes.

Ray came around the table and put his arms round her. She fell into his embrace and started to cry, he just held her tightly. Offering his comfort and support, he kissed her on the head and held her closer. "Babe, don't cry. There is nothing to cry about, we are okay."

"What if you can't get on with the kids and they piss you off, what if you decide this is not what you want?"

She looked up at him and the sight of her crying made a lump come to his throat. This woman who loved him very much and would do anything for him was hurt. He swallowed hard and kissed her forehead, saying, "Diane, I love you and am not going to leave you."

"Promise me." she said through her tears.

"I promise you!" He smiled and winked; she smiled back and squeezed him tight.

"I thought I was going to lose you," she said.

"No, you don't get shut of me that easily."

"I don't want to get shut of you, not ever," she said, looking into his eyes.

"In about fifty years you might regret saying that."

"Fifty? You should be so lucky." She smiled and wiped the tears from her face. "Cheeky sod."

"Is Amber alright now?"

"She is still stirring a bit in her sleep, she should be okay though."

"Well, you stay with her tonight. Go back up there and get some sleep and tomorrow I will let you cook me a big breakfast. How's that?" he said jokingly.

"No, you can cook breakfast for a change. Are you sure it's okay that I stay with Amber, just for tonight?" Diane had stopped crying and calmed a lot, getting her composure back.

"Yeah, of course it is. You sleep with her and make sure she is okay. I am going to make a tea and watch a little television. Now, stop worrying and go get cleaned up, or I will take you over my knee and give you a nice spanking."

"When you're big enough." She smiled, stood up and kissed him gently on the lips.

"I'm big enough for you, babe."

"Oh, we are bragging now, are we?" she said with wide eyes.

"You wouldn't like it on your nose as a wart."

"You're disgusting sometimes," she said shaking her head with a smile.

"I thought you liked it that way."

"We are going to be alright, aren't we Ray?" Her concern suddenly came back into her voice.

"Yes, babe, of course we are. It will be hard until I get work and you start to get paid, but we will manage. I don't want you to get upset about it, it will make you ill and do you no good." He took her hand and gave it a reassuring squeeze.

"That's alright then. I don't like falling out and arguing. You should never go to sleep on an argument, my dad always said that."

"My dad always said, 'Get out and find a bloody job, lad.'"

"I'm serious. We should always sort things out and not let them fester."

"Okay, you're right. I know what you mean."

"How is your hand?" she asked, looking at the plaster.

"It's okay, not too serious. I will live, I think."

"Do you want me to take a look at it?"

"Yes, and after that you can look at my hand as well," he grinned at her.

"Oh shut up. You're sex mad." She playfully punched him on the arm, then, smiling down at him, she sighed.

"You go to bed, you look shattered, darling."

"I am. I have had no sleep since Amber woke us up." She kissed him again and left the kitchen while he watched her go. When she looked back at him from the door, he blew her a kiss and she did the same back to him, then she went upstairs.

Bodie had been watching it all from his position on the floor. Ray tapped his leg and Bodie came over to his side and Ray rubbed him while he listened to the bathroom door open, and a few minutes later close again, Diane finally returning to Amber's room. He knew she was tired, he could tell the way she looked, and knew it would not be long before she went back to sleep.

He watched the television for about twenty minutes, then he went under the stairs and got the ouija board, disappearing back into the living room and closing the door behind him.

CHAPTER 14

The next morning Amber brought a cup of tea up to Ray, putting it down carefully on the small table by the bed, and she pushed him, saying gently, "Ray, wake up." He stirred a little, not entirely asleep. He turned and looked at her smiling at him, she was all dressed and ready for the day. She pushed her glasses up then then pointed to the tea by the side of the bed.

"Thanks," he said, looking at it. He sat up and yawned widely.

"I hope it is alright for you, I made it myself," she said proudly, looking at the tea mug.

"Well, let's have a taste then," Ray said, picking it up and taking a sip. He swallowed and smiled at her, nodding his head in agreement.

"It is okay for you?" she asked.

"Lovely, thank you," he told her putting it back down.

"Oh, good, I am glad." She sat on the bed and looked at Ray, smiling shyly.

"You alright, Amber, after your nightmare?" he asked carefully.

"Yes I am fine now, but it was not very nice." She frowned and shook her head.

"Can you talk about it?"

"If you want, but it was not very nice, Ray." Her eyes screwed up a little and she seemed to cringe at the thought of it.

"Just tell me what you saw," he said.

"Ugly people and bodies in the kitchen, blood all over the floor and walls. I didn't like it at all, it felt as if I was there. It was very scary."

"Is that all you saw? Did any of these ugly people say anything to you?" Ray took his tea once more and drank a bit more of it, while looking at Amber.

"It was as if I was watching and they didn't know I was there. They had very ugly faces and they were chopping at this body on the kitchen table. There were other bodies on the walls, I think. I can't really remember, it is too scary. Oh, there was a dead dog too, it was laid out across the back door, I think. Why did I have that dream, Ray? I won't have it again, will I?" Her voice became worried and she looked concerned.

"No, you won't have it again, I don't think. Anyway, dreams can't hurt you, and your Mum is only in the next room if you need her."

"And you? You would help me, wouldn't you Ray?"

"Yeah, I would help you." He smiled and drank some more of his tea.

"Can I have a hug?" she asked politely. He lifted his arm and she came under it and hugged him, he put his arm around her and gave her a little hug back.

"Amber, this bloke goes in and robs a bank then turns to the man at the desk and says 'Did you see me rob this bank?' 'Yes' says the man, so he shoots him. Then he asks another man, 'Did you see me rob this bank?' And the man says, 'Yes', so he shoots him as well. Then he turns to this couple and says to the man 'Did you see me rob this bank?' And the man says, 'No, but my wife did.'"

There was silence for a moment, then Amber looked up at him, waiting, finally asking him innocently, "Is that it?"

"Yes" Ray smiled at her.

"Did the police get the man?"

"Pardon?"

"The man who robbed the bank and shot those people?"

"No, Amber. It's a joke, love."

"Oh, right. I don't get it."

"You will when you get older, in more ways than one, I should think."

"Your jokes don't make sense, Ray. Why don't you find some funny jokes?"

"Yeah, I'm going to have to try, eh?"

"Yes I think you should. Anyway, I have to go to help Mum, so I will see you later." She got off the bed with a spring and marched out of the room while Ray finished his tea and slowly rubbed his hand, seeing that the wound was healing and closing up.

He lifted himself up and sat on the edge of the bed. Looking at his mobile, he noticed it was very low on battery, so he took the charger from the side of the bed and plugged this in, then the phone into the charger.

He went into the bathroom and had a shower, changed the plaster on his hand, got dressed and went downstairs, walking into the kitchen where Amber and Diane were making cakes. Diane turned and smiled at him and they both walked to each other and kissed. Amber looked, shook her head and carried on stirring her mixture.

"What you two up to then?" Ray enquired loudly enough that both Amber and Diane heard him.

"We are making cakes," Diane proudly announced to the whole kitchen.

"Yes and you can have one when they are ready," Amber said without turning around.

"Great stuff," Ray said, then held Diane closer to him, kissing her again.

"Good morning," she said with a smile. Her old ways had returned and Ray was happy for it.

"You okay?" he asked softly.

"Yes, I am fine. Sorry about last night."

"Don't mention it, we can make up for it tonight." He smiled and put both his hands on her buttocks and squeezed, pulling her closer to kiss her again.

"Excuse me, I could do with a hand here, please," Amber said, turning and looking at them both with a questioning eye.

"Sorry, Miss," Ray said, winking at Diane. He went over to Bodie and petted him where he was laying by the back door. Opening this, they both went out, while Diane went back to her daughter to help with the cakes.

Bodie and Ray headed down to the lake, Bodie marked his spots and explored, as usual, while Ray stood and looked out across the lake. He wondered what lay under the water, what secrets it held. He stared for sometime before he turned and looked back up to the house and around the area. He was in deep thought about something, playing with an idea in his head.

Bodie went to the water's edge and looked out the across the lake, becoming still and quiet for a moment before quickly dashing to where Ray was standing. "You alright, boy?" Ray asked, looking down at his dog who looked up with his ears back. Ray reached down and comforted him with a pat on the head.

They both walked a little along the edge of the lake, then moved on around and walked back in the direction of the barns. They walked past the tree Ray had fired his crossbow into, then up between the two barns and out to the front of the house.

It was going to be a nice day, the sun was getting up and the heat was rising. They both walked across the front of the house and down the other side and back around to the back door. They went back in and Ray changed the water in Bodie's bowl, then went and got him some food while Bodie had a long drink of nice cool fresh water.

They both could smell something, the cakes that Amber and Diane had made. They were in the oven baking. After enjoying the delicious aroma, Ray walked into the main room and sat on the settee. Diane came downstairs and walked into the room. Seeing Ray, she smiled and stood in front of him.

"Anything you would like?" she said with a cheeky smile.

"Oh yeah, a nice cup of tea, please," he said with an equally cheeky smile.

"What are we going to do today?" she asked.

"I thought we all could go into town to do some food shopping and then I will go to the job centre and have a look for some work" he announced.

"Oh yeah, that would be great" Diane said with wide pleased eyes, it was a great idea and something she really wanted to do. She sat beside him on the settee and took his hand in hers.

"Well, after a cup of tea, that is," Ray added.

"Coming right up," she said, standing back up.

"Bet you say that to all the boys."

"Only the handsome ones, lover," she joked, leaving to go and make his cup of tea.

As she was leaving, she passed Amber as she came into the room and stood by the window. She looked back over her shoulder and said to Ray, "My cakes are in the oven."

"Yes, I can smell them. I bet they are going to be very nice."

"I have not made cakes for a while, but I think they will be ok. I will let you have one if you like, when they are ready."

"That's good then, thanks. Amber, have you heard the one about the woman who went to a sex shop and asked for a vibrator? When the assistant wagged his finger and said, 'Come this way,' she replied, 'If I came that way, I wouldn't need a vibrator.'"

"What's a vibrator?" she asked with a blank expression.

"It doesn't matter," he said, smiling.

"Okay, I'm going to the loo," she announced, leaving the room. A few minutes later Diane came back in with two mugs of tea, she gave one to Ray and kept the other one, sitting next to him on the settee.

"Thanks, love," he said, taking a sip of the hot tea.

"We don't have any biscuits," she told him.

"Have to get some today. My old credit card is going to have to take a bashing."

"We are running a bit short of money, Ray."

"Don't worry, I will get some work of some sort soon. We will be okay, I still have some savings and that should get us through."

"It will be better when I get paid, but I have to work a month in hand, so it is going to be some time before I have any."

"Stop fretting, babe, we will be fine. I won't let us starve."

"No, I know, but I would like some money coming in all the same."

"Tell you what, and I don't want any arguments. Sod money, we are going out shopping today and then tonight I will take you all out for a meal. We will go to a pub that sells grub or something, there must be one somewhere nearby."

"That would be bloody great," she smiled and nodded her head excitedly in agreement.

"Yeah it would. Then we can come home and you can have your wicked way with me."

"Oh promises, promises. We are going to alright, aren't we Ray?" her voice seemed a little concerned and worried all of a sudden.

"Of course we are, babe. It has been a very trying and stressful time moving in here and doing it up, but we are getting there now, babe," he reassured her.

"We are settling now, aren't we? Getting there?"

"Sure are, sexy" he winked and smiled at her. She smiled back and winked at him.

They finished their tea, Amber's cakes were taken out and left to cool on a tray, and then they all got ready to have a day out. Even Tommy seemed happy for a change. As they were getting ready, Ray told Amber a joke that she didn't get, Diane made sure that the children were ready, Ray did a few quick checks on his car and made sure that the place was locked up after giving Bodie one last stroke.

They all were seated in Ray's car less then forty-five minutes later, all seat belts on, doors closed, engine started and then they pulled away slowly out of the courtyard and through the gates, heading for town and a family day out.

The house was silent, still and empty, except for Bodie. He was lying on the kitchen floor, relaxing on his side with his legs stretched out. Suddenly something startled him, his ears sprang up and he was on his feet in less than two seconds. He growled; something was wrong, he sensed it, but did not know what it was. He stood and looked into the hallway for a moment. His eyes fixed on the stairs and he growled louder, edging forward slowly. He stopped in the kitchen doorway, listening and looking.

Without warning, he began to bark savagely, ferociously at the stairs. The hair on his back was up and he was baring his teeth. He was a formidable sight, a force to be reckoned with. He barked at the stairs relentlessly, a savage animal, protective and vicious, he was scared and showing his anger and strength to mask his fear.

He was not the only one who was upset and worried. In the small barn, curled up and shivering, was the small weak thing that lived there. It was shaking with fear, curled up tightly into a ball, whimpering like a small terrified puppy.

The sound then came from the woods, a howling, a long howling. Bodie heard it and it made him bark more, the barn dweller heard it and it made him cry with fear. Something was wrong, very wrong, and the animals could sense it more than a human could.

Bodie stood alert watching from the kitchen into the front room. He was not sure what it was, this strange presence, it was something he could neither see nor smell, he just felt it, knew it was there. He had not experienced anything like it before, even the feeling he got in the woods did not match this.

Suddenly the place seemed to be void of time and noise. The howling stopped and it was deadly quiet around the house, inside and out. No breeze, no sound, nothing at all. The place could have been a photo you were looking at, no atmosphere, no reality and no life.

Oblivious to all this was Ray, Diane and her children. They were driving into town and the mood in the car was a happy one. The windows were down and a nice cool breeze was blowing through the car. Diane was in the front passenger seat with her hand on Ray's knee while the two children sat in the back seat, looking out of the window.

"Am I right in saying there is a postal sorting office somewhere down here?" Ray asked no one in particular.

"Yes there is, about a mile down the road. I remember passing it the other day," Diane replied.

"I will pop in and see if they can tell me why we are not getting any mail," he said. They drove to the small sorting office and Ray parked, then he smiled and got out of the car. They all watched him disappear into a small, red glass door with a sign "Enquiries" on the top of it. Diane settled back into her seat.

"Mum?" asked Amber.

"Yes, love?" Diane said.

"What is a vibrator?" she innocently and very calmly asked. Tommy instantly started to giggle while Diane, shocked, was speechless for a moment. Turning in her seat, she looked at her with an open mouth, before eventually saying, "I beg your pardon? What made you ask that question?"

"A woman goes and asks for one and wiggles her finger or something" she said, confused.

"Is this one of Ray's jokes?" she asks, almost relieved.

"Yes, but I didn't get it."

"What is the joke?" Tommy asked interestedly.

"She wiggles her finger and says I wouldn't want one or something." She shakes her head; she was getting confused and could not remember the joke at all.

Diane had to smile to her self , but did not let her children see. When she had got her face straight and serious again she turned back and looked at them saying, "Calm down, it is not funny. I will have to have a word with him about his jokes."

They all settle into silence again and waited for Ray to return, which took some time. They saw him come out of the same door he went in, shaking his head. He looked annoyed and in his hand were several letters. He got into the car and handed the letters to Diane saying,   "No mail gets delivered to that address, it has to be collected. He wanted proof of who I was, but like I said, if you don't bloody deliver me mail, I don't have the proof I live there do I, anyway I had a long form to fill in and I finally got the mail."

"Why the hell don't they deliver to us?" Diane asked, confused.

"Probably too far for the postman to come. I don't know, he wouldn't give me a straight answer, bloody pen-pushing wanker."

"Well we have some bills and bank statements and some stuff we have been waiting for here," Diane tells him as she looks through the letters.

"What is this world coming to, there used to be one day a year the post didn't deliver and that was Christmas, now they won't even walk to your sodding door," Ray said, starting the car back up. He reversed out of the small car park and into the main road, checked both ways, then pulled off again heading into the town.

Diane carefully checked through the mail, opening a few of the letters and just stacking other, less important ones, under the pile on her knee.

The mood changed back to a happy one a few moments later, after Ray had got over the incident in the sorting office. They headed into town and he parked in the centre, they paid the parking fee and all went off into town. Diane was happy because they were out as a family unit, this is what she liked and wanted the most.

Holding Ray's hand, she walked proudly and happily with him, and with her children close by, she could not have been happier. They visited the local careers office and Ray looked for a job. He talked to a woman and explained the situation, he left all his details and told them he would be in touch. It was a half-hearted attempt, but at least it was a start. They did some window shopping and had a nice family day out around the town.

Later that evening, Ray suggested they go for a meal at a pub before they went home, refusing to take no for an answer. When they got back into the car, he drove off, looking for a pub that sold food.

The day had been a total success and Diane was very comfortable. Ray seemed more at ease, back to his old self, and her kids had been laughing. At this moment she could not feel any better. Ray was looking for a family pub that sold food and he decided on the Fox and Hound.

It was an old-looking pub, but it was local, and a long sign announced that it sold good old-fashioned food. He made his way to it and parked in the small, but tidy, car park. The place was stone built and had been here for years, you could tell by the age of the stone and roof. Ray looked up and smiled, he always did at a grey slate roof. It reminded of his dad putting them on when he was a child, and how he told him " That will be there until the house falls down now, lad."

The place was warm and cosy, a real fire roared in the main room, the carpet was soft under the foot, it was quiet and well maintained and Diane liked it instantly. Ray walked up to the bar and looked across at the man behind it, he was reading a paper sat on a small stool. The place was almost half full and people were drinking, a few had empty plates in front of them, obviously having already eaten their food and now settled into a drink and a chat.

"Shop," Ray said, looking at the small balding man, who looked up, startled for a moment. He then put the paper down and walked over. He smiled courteously and said in a voice that didn't suit his size, so deep and powerful was it, "Good evening, sir, what will it be?"

"Pint of lager, half a lager and two cokes please" Ray told him in a monotone voice.

"Right away," he said as he went and fetched two glasses and began to pour the drinks.   He smiled at Diane, who smiled back and asked, "Could we have a meal as well, please?"

"Yes, the menus are on the table. Just order at the bar when you're ready and it will be brought to you. Make a note of your table number when you're ordering," he said, smiling very politely.

Handing the pint and half to Ray, the barman went and got the two cokes. Ray handed these to Diane who went and sat down at a table with them, followed by her children. The table she chose was out of the way and around a corner, not in full sight of the rest of the pub. She knew Ray didn't like people watching him eat.

"You just passing then, sir?" asked the barman as he put he drinks on the bar.

"No, we have bought the farm house up the way there," said Ray, pointing in the direction he thought their house was.

"What, the old farm house?" the barman asked, looking concerned.

"Yes, do you know it?" Ray asked.

"I know it, sir," he looked away and his mood changed immediately. He looked around, not wanting to look back at Ray, who was staring at him.

"How much do I owe you?" Ray eventually asked.

"That will be five pound twenty, please." The smile and friendly look had gone from his face, replaced with a frown and a look of worry.

Ray handed him the exact money, it was taken without eye contact being made and no more was said. Ray left the bar not letting the incident faze him at all. He took two drinks at

first then came back for the two cokes and, while Diane and her children were busy looking at

the menu, Ray was sipping his drink.

He could sense the people talking and whispering, he looked behind him and caught a

couple looking over at them, but their gaze shifted as Ray stared back. The news had gone

through the place so rapidly, it was almost instantaneous. He did not tell Diane.

"What are you having, babe?" she said with a smile.

"Steak and chips with all the trimmings, and leave the horns on," Ray replied, smiling.

"Can we afford it?" she asked quietly.

"Don't worry, it is my treat, anything you want." Ray smiled.

She smiled widely and mouthed 'Thank you' back to him.

It was not long before they have all chosen what they wanted and Ray walked to the

bar to order. He was met with the same reaction as before, people looking at him as he

walked past, the whispers and the look of confused fear in people's faces.

He managed to get through ordering without saying anything to the young girl who

refused to even look at him as he ordered the food. He kept calm and ignored them all.

Sitting back down, he looked at Tommy and asked, "What do you call a lesbian

dinosaur?"

"I don't know, Ray" Tommy said.

"A lickalotapuss."

Tommy giggled and Diane smiled to herself, she shook her head and said nothing.

Amber's confused look told him she did not get the joke.

"It's nice in here," Diane said, looking round.

"Yes, it's okay. Pleasant," Ray agreed.

The food arrived shortly afterwards, the cutlery was put down and each plate given to the right person by two young girls, who asked for confirmation on who was eating what. No smiles, no customary 'Enjoy your meal', nothing but straight, basic service.

After they had gone Diane looked at Ray disappointedly and said "The place is nice, but service with a smile is shit."

"Sod them, they're young. Just enjoy, eh," Ray said.

They started their meal and it was very good food. Diane was so happy at this simple outing as a family that she thought the food tasted even better because Ray had treated them all to it.

"What are you eating, Amber?" Ray asked her.

"I have chicken," she said, after swallowing the mouthful that was being chewed.

"What side of a chicken has the most feathers?" Ray asked her.

"I don't know," she said, after thinking intensely for a moment.

"The outside," Ray said with a smile while eating a chip from his plate.

Amber looked at him, her face smirked and cracked, then she laughed out loud and bent over, giggling at the remark.

"Hey, she got one of my jokes!" Ray announced to the rest of the table. This monumental event had to be shared.

They all laughed, Amber was getting hysterical and it made everyone else laugh at her infectious chuckle. It was several minutes before they calmed down, all taking a drink more or less at the same time.

The meal was a great success and they all enjoyed it. After the plates were taken away, Ray went and got more drinks. He got Diane a gin and tonic, this was her favourite and she had not had one for so long. Her eyes lit up when he brought it to her. They drank and had a very merry time.

He bought Diane more drinks than she could take and she became a little tipsy and the children laughed, enjoying them selves immensely. It was an adventure to be in a pub, seeing their mum laugh and be happy, and it was funny watching her getting a little drunk.

Ray stayed sober and in control, he could sense the growing atmosphere in the place against them. He looked at the clock on the wall next to the toilet sign and stood up, stretching, then saying, "Just going to point Percy at the porcelain, won't be long, about nine inches."

Diane laughed and rocked back and her children did the same, although they didn't know what they were laughing at. It was more at their mother than anything else.

The toilet was well kept and clean. Ray went to the urinal and relived himself, next to a young man. He looked away from Ray's gaze as he walked in and was still looking away now, then the curiosity got the better of him and he looked at Ray.

"You looking at something?" Ray said.

"No," he said, looking away quickly. He then looked back saying, "You have bought the old farm house, haven't you?"

"Yes, what of it? Is that a crime around here?"

"Well, you could say it is, in a way. The place should never have been sold." He zipped up his trousers and left, he didn't even wash his hands. Ray also finished and went to the sink, he washed his hands and looked at himself in the mirror above the sink, standing there for several minutes just staring into his own eyes, questioning and searching.

He knew what they all thought, he knew why they were acting like they did, and in a way he didn't blame them, if anyone was to blame it was him. He searched his soul for an answer, for a reason, his eyes stared back at him and he was emotionless. After this, he blinked and brought himself back into reality and to his own consequences.

***

It was dark when they left the pub, Diane giggling at nothing and everything, her children finding her very amusing and Ray playing along with the whole scene. He soon was driving them back home, the night was damp, rain was in the air. He drove carefully, the headlights lit the way and he concentrated on the road ahead.

Diane started to sing a song on the way home, she was so happy and wanted everyone to know it. The children, although tired, joined in with pleasure and the car's atmosphere was buzzing.

CHAPTER 15

They were soon turning up the lane that led to their house. Ray slowed his pace and headed up straight and true, the large powerful engine easing them safely on their way. Despite the noise of the car and the singing, Ray still could hear it. He looked to the side, trying not to alarm the others, the rest of the car was too busy singing to notice, but he could hear it well.

The howling from the woods. It was not constant, but it was there and more than one howl, more than one thing making it, several different tones, and pitches. Some deeper than others, some more rough, but still distinctively howling from the wood.

He put his foot down slightly to get past more quickly, hoping no one else could hear it, and he managed to do what he wanted. He got them into the yard at the front of the house without any of them hearing what he had. He stopped the car outside the front of the house.

"Straight to bed then, kids, it's late," he said, turning off the engine.

They all got out of the car and Ray locked it up while Diane came around and linked arms with him. She was smiling, feeling giddy, and he helped her to the door, opening it and flicking the light on. The kids ran in and went straight upstairs, they were tired and wanted to go to bed.

He helped Diane up the stairs, she was smiling at him but saying nothing. He managed to push the bedroom door open with his foot and got her in, all her weight was on his arm now as she became more and more dependent on him. He man-handled her to the bed and she flopped onto it, still smiling, but out like a light.

He walked back out of the room and closed the door, knowing that she would be out for the night, he noticed the kids had gone to bed also. He went downstairs and wondered where Bodie was. He called him and then heard a slight bark come from the kitchen. The door was shut and Bodie was inside.

He opened the door and greeted his dog, wondering why the door was shut. He disregarded this and let the dog out the back door, watching as he disappeared into the night for a few minutes. He changed the water for him and dropped him some food into his dish for when he returned.

He suddenly felt cold, the house seemed very cold and damp. He then walked out of the kitchen, noticing that all the doors were shut, doors that he didn't remember closing that morning when they left. He walked to the living room and opened the door and, when turned on the light, what greeted him sent a cold shiver down his spine.

In the middle of the room on the floor was the ouija board, set up and ready, the planchette sitting in the middle of the board. He knew he had put this safely away the last time he used it, and it was most definitely not there that morning. He looked around the room, nothing else seemed out of place.

For a moment he did not know what to do, he looked behind him, then back into the room. Luckily Diane had flaked out and the kids were in their room, he would not have liked to have had to explain this away, not that he could explain it. He slowly walked up to the board, then he knelt down and tried to pick the planchette up, but it was solid it would not move, it seemed to be glued, riveted to the ouija board. He pulled at it, tried to push it, but it still would not move. He noticed his hands shaking slightly, so he took a deep breath and tried once more, but it was no good. The thing was solid and would not budge.

He tried to pick the board up from the floor, but the same applied, it would not move. He did not know what it was, but something was holding them tightly down and he was not able to move them. Standing, he kicked at the wooden planchette with the heel of his shoe. It was rock solid, like kicking a brick wall. He knelt down and placed his fingers under the wooden edge and tried to prize the thing upwards off the board, his fingers slipped off causing pain to run through his fingertips.

Cursing, he left the room, returning moments later with a claw hammer which he placed under the planchette as he tried again. Pulling hard on the hammer's shaft, he gave it all his strength, but still nothing moved. He took the hammer and hit the thing on the top, hoping to crack the wood or smash it, but nothing was working.

Looking around in desperation, he did not know what to do. He noticed a chill come over the room, a moist feeling and he felt his body shiver with the wet air he was breathing. The room seemed to be in a void, a silent and unnatural atmosphere that he felt uncomfortable with. He looked at the board when suddenly there was a deafening crack in the air, like a whip.

He ducked instinctively, holding his ears and backed away, not understanding what was going on. The crack was ear-shattering and he was sure it would have woken the household up. But nothing happened after that; he looked to the door and saw Bodie just sitting there looking at him.

He looked back at the board and did not know why, but knew he would now be able to pick it up. He knelt down and picked it up with the planchette without any problem. He wasted no time and ran for the back door, out and down to the lake, his way only lit by the moonlight. Bodie was following in silence.

When he got to the edge of the water, he took the board in his right hand and pulled his arm back, throwing it with all his might as far into the lake as possible. Next he took the planchette and did the same, throwing it far out into the lake and hearing it hit the water out far in front of him.

He stood motionless for a few moments breathing heavily. He reached down and stroked Bodie on the head as he came and sat next to him, looking out into the dark water in front of them. The water could be heard slightly moving, but suddenly it seemed to vibrate; ripples were coming over the surface, starting from the centre and moving out to the edges of the lake. Bodie stood and backed up a few paces, he growled, not liking this at all.

Ray watched and listened, he was not too keen on the situation himself. He looked up quickly as he heard a howl from the woods. It was a strong long howl and he swallowed, fear creeping into his normally steady state. He had become unnerved, shaking and sweating. He did not like what was going on, he did not like what he had done, and he did not know what would happen because of it.

"Bodie, come on, lad," he said and went hurriedly back to the house. They both went in and Ray locked and secured the doors, he made sure of this twice. He looked around and then bedded Bodie down, then he went up the stairs and into the bathroom where he splashed water over his face and stared at himself in the mirror once more.

He came into the bedroom a little later. He went to the window and looked out, but the impenetrable darkness robbed him of the ability to see anything. He looked at Diane who looked happy with a little grin on her face, but was out to the world. The alcohol had taken effect and knocked her out of the conscious state until morning.

Ray got into bed, but he did not sleep that night. He kept catching the noise of a howl from the woods, he kept thinking he heard something in the house, something outside, his imagination was playing havoc with him and there was nothing he could do about it. He got up several times and looked out of the window and, eventually, the daylight came into the sky, and a new day was here.

***

Amber was the first one up, she came down looking rough but wide awake. Ray was standing at the back door, looking out towards the lake, he knew she had come down but did not acknowledge it; he was preoccupied looking across to the stretch of water at the back. She smiled at him as she walked past, even though he was facing the other way.

She went and got herself some cereal and ate this at the kitchen table, got a drink, then put the pots into the sink. She looked at Ray and said. "I'm just going out for a stroll, Ray, won't be long."

"Okay, but do not go near the lake, alright?" Ray insisted.

She nodded and put her shoes on, going out the front door and walked round to the barns. Bodie was in the back garden, staying close to Ray. He knew something was very wrong and wanted to be near his master at all times, his alpha male was worried and he knew he had to be there for him, had to do what was needed, and he was ready to do so.

Amber was not going anywhere in particular, she just fancied a little walk. She came to the small barn and stood at the entrance, she looked in and tried to imagine what it would look like with her pony in there. The dream had drifted somewhat now, because she had come to realise that Ray had done no work on it at all and the money was not good. But she still wished and hoped as she slowly walked into the barn.

From above the red, blood-shot eyes were watching her with hawk-like intensity. Not like before with a hint of fear and dread, but with hate and dislike, almost with a lust to cause her pain. The eyes followed her and the mouth of the thing watching was beginning to drool, drip with saliva and it made strange little noises as it watched her every move.

Amber stopped because she thought she had heard something, she looked around and then up, searching the barn. She looked right at the spot from where the eyes were staring at her, but she did not recognise them and looked past the spot. Turning, she skipped along the barn and then out of the entrance again, humming a little tune to herself.

The eyes followed her and it dashed to the side of the barn, peering through a gap in the wooden construction where it could see out into the yard. It continued watched Amber as she skipped back out towards the open field. The noise it was making was not human, could not be called normal, it was a noise like it was in pain, a croaking from its throat. Its mouth was open and its tongue was hanging out, saliva dripping down. Its hands were held up near its face as it hunched over, keeping its eyes on Amber, watching her all the while she was in sight.

She was oblivious to all this and did not know she was being watched so intensely, with so much hate and venom directed towards her. She pushed her glasses up with her one finger, then pulled at the jeans she was wearing to pull them up.

The morning was nice and clear and she stood in the field looking up at a small bird as it was rising high in the sky. It hovered there and started to sing its tune while she watched and smiled at it. She found that she had come to like this place more and more every day. Even if she did not get her pony.

Walking back towards the house, she thought of her new school and the new friends she will meet. Her mother had reassured her of the possibilities and now she was not too bothered about going. She was even looking forward to it, they could have a nice time with her new friends here, playing out in the field and the barn and the lake.

She knelt down and picked a few little flowers that were growing near her feet; she picked these and started to arrange them in her hands as she walked back towards the house. She would put them in a glass of water and put them on the side to brighten up the kitchen, she thought. Her mum liked flowers and these looked very nice, little blue ones with a hint of yellow. She was not sure what they were, but they looked nice and that is all that mattered.

She marched back into the house and to the kitchen where she took a glass and half filled it with water and placed her flowers in it, putting them on the side as she had planned. Then she went into the main room and turned on the television, sitting in front of it to watch a program about wildlife in the African national parks.

Sarah was just opening her eyes, she got them adjusted to the light, and saw Ray looking out of the window, watching out towards the lake. She stretched and yawned, then wished she hadn't; her head started to pound and the sick feeling hit her full throttle. "Oh

God, I'm ill," she said, rolling back on her side and gently resting her head back on the pillow so as not to shift it too much or too quickly.

"Morning, piss head," Ray said, still looking out of the window.

"How much did I drink last night?" she asked delicately.

"Too much, but you enjoyed yourself and that is what counts." He came from the window and sat gently next to her on the bed, smiled at how ill she looked, her poor, helpless face.

"It's your fault, I blame you," she quietly told him.

"Would you like some bacon and eggs and fried tomatoes for breakfast, dear?" he jested.

"Sod off. No I would not and no, I am never drinking again." She moaned as she moved her head a little too fast, making herself sick.

"You could never take your drink, could you?"

"If you knew that, why did you let me drink that much, you shit?" she said, smiling at him.

"Well you didn't have that much really, but you only live once."

"Thank God, I don't want to go through this again." she rolled over tentatively.

"I will leave you for a few hours and I will return when you have recovered." He gently kissed her on her forehead and quietly left the room. He went downstairs and into the living room.

He found Amber, who was absorbed in the television and did not turn to look at him as he said, "Amber, when Tommy gets up, tell him not to go near the lake, okay? I am just taking Bodie out."

"Can I come, please?" she asked.

"No, not this time. I just want to walk him a bit, okay? We will do something later."

"Okay, that's cool." She turned back and carried on watching the television.

Moments later Ray and Bodie were walking out of the house, across the yard and down toward the woods. Ray looked intense and Bodie's mood followed; they both knew something was not right, something was happening and it was not good. They walked down the road and headed off into the woods on the side, walking deeper into the trees. Bodie stayed close to his master, watching, listening, smelling, guarding.

They headed out to where Ray had fallen down the hole and, as they walked, Ray noticed they was no noise, nor movement of any kind. No birds, no animals, even the trees seemed to be menacing, almost accusing, the leaves unnaturally still. He looked down at Bodie whose black ears were pointed up, his gaze straight forward, his look ominous.

As they walked on, deeper into the trees, the air became thicker, more stagnant. It was harder to breath and harder to walk; it was much more tiring then usual. When they reached the spot they were after, Ray stood above the hole. It was as he feared, it was disturbed, moved, shifted, not as he left it.

Bodie growled, he was looking up into the trees above. Ray looked up, unable to see anything, although he knew something was there, watching. Bodie did not make mistakes like that.

"Come on, lad," Ray said and moved on, followed by his loyal dog. He walked a little further and noticed another hole, a smaller one, but this one was much fresher. It had not been there long and, though there was nothing in it, it was apparent that there had been. He looked around the woods and could see nothing, but his instinct told him he was being watched, and being watched by a legion of eyes. It was unnerving.

He decided that he had seen enough, in fact, he had seen too much. He headed back out of the woods and as he walked he noticed several other holes in the forest floor. Something seemed to have escaped from the ground, something had dug its way out, something had come back.

His pace quickened, he was walking fast and Bodie was trotting to keep up. He didn't like this any more than his master. They were soon running, running out of the woods, running onto the road, and running back to the house. They went around so as not to be visible from the front, over some shrubbery and down the back, stopping at the lake.

Bodie sat and looked out across the water as did Ray, who was out of breath from the exercise. He looked out across the same water and saw the ripples intensifying, a vibration was still causing the water to move, something under it was moving, shuddering, shaking.

Bodie stood and went to the water's edge, bowed his head and smelt the water, looking deep into it. Ray came next to him and knelt down, reaching out to touch the cold water. It was unnaturally cold, almost like ice, but it was not winter. He tried to wipe it from his fingers, but it would not shift. He rubbed his fingers on his jeans, but they stayed cold.

He stood back up and pulled Bodie back, then began rubbing his hands together the way you do in winter to keep them warm, but to no avail. His fingers were cold and staying cold, very cold. He clenched a fist and tucked his fingers into the palm of his hand, and cupped this hand in his other one; he wanted the coldness to go from his fingers.

He noticed the ripples were getting stronger, fiercer. He did not know what it was or what to do, nothing had prepared him for this and he was at a loss to know what to think or how to react. He looked back up towards the house and had to make a decision, he had to work out what the outcome of this, what ever it was going to be.

Walking back up to the house, he shook his hand. He was beginning to get the feeling back into his fingers, they didn't feel as dead, more alive and back to normal.

It was several hours before Diane finally got out of bed, she slowly went to the bathroom and tried to be sick, but it was not coming. She had a wash and went to the toilet, got some loose clothes on and headed downstairs. She made herself a coffee and took some painkillers, then she sat at the table holding her head.

Amber came in and sat across from her. She smiled and looked at the flowers in the glass on the side, then she looked back at her mother saying, "I have picked you some flowers, Mum."

"Oh thank you, love. They are very nice," Diane managed to say, without looking up.

"They are over there, in that glass, I have put them in water," Amber pointed to the glass on the side so her mother would know where to look.

"Very nice love, thank you." Diane took a sip of her coffee and rested the mug back down softly on the table, to make as little noise as possible.

"They were in the field, the only thing growing there. It's strange, really, you would think there would be lots of flowers growing wild, wouldn't you?"

"Ermm, yeah," Diane was struggling with this and had to try very hard.

"Let your mum be, Amber, she is a little ill," Ray told her from the kitchen door, where he stood watching them.

"Okay, that's cool." She happily got up and went up to her room.

Ray came and sat across from Diane, he had a little smile on his face. "A little delicate are we, love?" he asked sarcastically.

"Bollocks. This is your fault," she mumbled, not taking her gaze from her mug of coffee.

"I suppose mad, passionate sex is out of the question then?"

"Not unless you want to kill me off."

"Why don't you go and get a bit of fresh air?"

She nodded carefully and slowly stood, quietly walking to the back door. Opening this, she breathed a deep breath of clean air and let it out slowly. Ray came up behind her and put his arms around her waist, she fell back into him and closed her eyes. His embrace felt nice and warm and loving.

"You look a little better than you did this morning, anyway," he told her, gently kissing her on the back of the neck.

"Fuck, I must have looked pretty bad, then."

"No one has ever died of a hangover."

"There is always a first time." She yawed and stretched her arms out, then snuggled back into her man, she felt better already and tilted her head back so Ray could kiss the side of her neck.

He kisses her slowly and she shuddered as he did so, this turned her on, but she was in no state to do anything about it, so pulled away and tilted her head the other way to stop him. "Did you enjoy last night?" he asked, stroking her hair lovingly.

"Yes it was lovely, nice meal, thank you. The people were a bit strange, though. I'm sure that they kept staring at us and whispering, or was that just me?"

"Well it's a small community and we are strangers, new faces."

"I don't know if it was that at all, it just seemed a bit strange. From what I can remember of it, anyway," she smiled to herself.

"So you don't remember what you did then?"

"Did? What?" She turned to face him with a confused look on her face.

"Showing your knickers and dancing on the table singing 'Save a Horse, Ride a Cowboy' at the top of your voice. The kids were terribly embarrassed, poor things, they will have to live that one down at school. We got kicked out."

"Oh sod off," she toy punched him in the stomach with a smile on her face. "'Save a Horse, Ride a Cowboy,' who sang that?" she asked.

"You, last night, at the top of your voice. And doing all the actions too. It turned me right on."

"No I didn't, stop telling lies." She smiled up at him and kissed him softly on the lips.

"Okay then, you didn't, you just did a pole dance on the bar."

"Sod off." She looked at him and a frown came across her face. "Are you okay, love? You look a little worried, not your normal self."

"Yeah I'm fine, just a little tired, I suppose." He smiled a reassuring smile.

"Are you sure? Have you had any breakfast?"

"No, I'm not hungry. Do you want some?"

"No, I'm fine, except for the thumping head and sick feeling, that is."

"Well you must be better than you were. Why don't you go and lay down for a bit?"

"No I'm up now, it will wear off. I might go for a stroll in the woods or somewhere."

"NO! I mean, no, you can't go in there, babe, not in your state. It wouldn't be safe."

"What do you mean? What is wrong, Ray?" She knew something was bothering him.

"Darling, nothing is wrong. Now come and show me them moves you were doing last night at the lap dance club." He smiled again and gave her a lascivious wink.

"Oh, you sexy bastard, if I was not so ill, I would have you up them stairs and shag the arse off ya." She smiled and gave him a hug, she was feeling better already. Holding onto her man, she closed her eyes for a moment and just relished the moment of being with him and being happy.

The day started with her feeling ill, but it was going to end with smiles, love and sex, she was going to make sure of that. Ray was looking out across to the lake as she hugged him; he was keeping his fear from her, but he knew it was not going to last. Something was going to happen. The questions were what would happen and when

CHAPTER 16

Late that afternoon the sun had begun to drop from the sky. Tommy had finally gotten out of bed, Amber had been everywhere and into everything, and Diane had recovered enough to go about normally. Ray was still on watch with Bodie, but trying to hide it from everyone. The day had, to all who did not know, been uneventful, the night would soon be here and darkness would engulf them once again.

Ray walked into the living room with Bodie by his side. He saw Diane reading a book with Amber, then, going still, he asked, "Where's Tommy?"

"I think he went down to the lake to see if he could go fishing," Amber said.

"Fuck!" Ray shouted and dashed from the house, much to the surprise of Diane and Amber, who both jumped out of their seat and ran after him as he went, followed by Bodie.

Diane held out her hand to signal Amber to stay and then went off after Ray, calling after him. She ran from the house and caught sight of him and Bodie disappearing down towards the lake and she followed, confused and a little annoyed at the situation.

"Tommy, get back here," Ray shouted at him as he saw him standing at the lake's edge looking at the movement of the water, which was much more prominent now.

"Ray, look at the water, it is moving," Tommy said, turning to face him with a surprised look.

"Back to the house, lad, move. NOW!" he shouted.

Tommy flinched at the ferocity of Ray's words but he started to back up and away from the water.

Diane came dashing up, out of breath and looking angry. "What the hell is wrong?" she asked them, holding out her hands for an explanation.

"The water is moving, Mum." Tommy came up and stood next to her, putting an arm around her for comfort and support.

She looked out across the water and watched the ripples move the whole surface of the lake. "Ray, what the fuck is it? What is wrong" she searched his face for an answer. Gasping for air, Tommy started to shake, frightened, and held onto his mother more tightly.

Ray just looked at them and said nothing. He then turned his gaze back out to the water where he watched the strange phenomenon, but just did not know how to explain it. Their stalemated state was shattered by a terrified scream from Amber back at the house. They all looked up as she screamed a petrified scream again.

"Bodie, round," Ray ordered and the dog ran off to circle his way back. He knew what to do and just did the job. Ray then dashed past a confused and lost-looking Diane, as he did it bolted her into motion and she and Tommy followed.

Amber had come out of the house to follow her mother but she had the shock of her life when the barn dweller had grabbed her and threw her to the ground. She shrieked when she saw the hideous creature looking down at her, snarling and spitting.

By the time Ray reached her, the creature had its foot on Amber's head, pinning the terrified child to the ground. It had a rusty, six-inch held, pointed end first, into her ear, and the hammer it had in its other hand was raised ready to hit the nail home.

"HEY!" Ray shouted as he skidded to a halt about ten yards in front of them. The creature looked up and snarled and spat at him, threateningly and viciously. Amber stayed frozen to the spot, she dared not move and was just shaking with fear. She did not understand what was going on, what was happening.

Diane's fear was unprecedented, she had not seen anything like it. Tommy clung tightly to her and looked away, the sight of the thing repulsed and frightened him. Screaming, Diane looked to Ray for help, she was shaking and staring at her daughter who was shaking on the ground.

"It's okay, Amber. Stay calm," Ray said, edging forward little by little. The creature snarled at him as he did so, lifting the hammer higher and more threateningly as a warning for him to stop.

"What the fuck is it?" Diane screamed at Ray. He just held up his hand and tried in vain to calm her, while he continued to edge forward.

"Ray, stop, for God's sake!" screamed Diane, who was hysterical and shaking, riveted to the spot. Ray saw what he had been waiting for; out of the corner of his eye he noticed a black figure, crouching low and stealthy moving along the ground.

It was Bodie, he had come around the side and got into position, not far at all from the creature now. The creature became agitated and knew that it was trapped; it was looking for a way out. Drooling and wide-eyed, it searched around for a getaway, screeching as it did, its foot turning on Amber's head as it moved its gaze about its surroundings.

It was a stand-off and no one knew what to do for a moment. Amber then could stay quiet no longer, fear had struck her dumb, but a cry came out, then a whimper, then a scream, and another. Tommy started to cry and held onto his mum, burying his head into her, refusing to look at the scene unfolding before him.

The creature screamed at the top of its voice as it noticed the black figure crouched by its side. Bodie had been spotted.

"Bodie, on guard!" Ray commanded.

Bodie stood and edged forward, not taking his eyes off the creature in front of him as he snarled at him. He was now stood only a few feet away from the creature and Amber, Ray was about ten feet away from this. It was a tense situation; Amber sobbed uncontrollably, Bodie growled and was like a coiled spring, ready to pounce.

"Don't panic, Amber, Bodie will protect you." Ray tried to reassure Amber as he continued to edge forward. The tension had to snap, and it did, right there and then.

The creature started to bring the hammer down onto the head of the nail, to send it driving into Amber's ear and through into her brain. Diane screamed and tried to run forward but Tommy prevented it with his grasp. Ray dove forward at the same time. They all fell short, but, fortunately, it was Bodie who had judged it right.

He was a large powerful dog who moved with surprisingly great speed and grace. Before the creature could bring the hammer down, it was knocked off of Amber by the sheer weight of Bodie. He pinned the thing to the ground, snarling, baring his teeth only inches from the face of the inhuman creature below him.

Amber rolled over crying and sobbing, Diane broke lose of Tommy and dashed over to cup her daughter in her arms, and Ray came forward to stand over Bodie, looking down at the pathetic thing that his powerful dog had pinned to the ground. In total control, the dog watched and guarded his victim.

He could have quite easily of ripped it apart but he did not. He would only do that with the command of his master. The creature was whimpering and petrified, helpless and vulnerable. Its life was worth nothing and this mighty animal could take it in less then a second.

There was a second or two of confusion now, no one knew what to do or say, or understood what had happened or why. The mood was broken by Tommy's screaming. He pointed to the lake and yelled out then went running to his mother who cupped him in her right arm, while doing the same to Amber with her left.

Ray looked down to the lake to where Tommy had pointed. What he saw made his blood turn cold and a shiver run down his spine and back up again. "Into the house, now! Quickly!" Ray ordered.

Diane and her children ran blindly into the back door while Bodie still had the thing pinned. Ray came up to him and pulled him back and off with his collar then he signalled to the house. As Bodie looked up at his master, the creature got up and ran frantically into the house where it cowered into a corner in the front room, curled up and shaking.

Ray and Bodie followed. Ray shut the door and bolted it, then he went to the front and did the same, finally closing the shutters on the windows, securing them firmly.

"Ray, what the hell is going on?" Diane shouted at him as he walked past her in the hall and rechecked the back door. The children were shaking and clinging on to their mother as if their life depended on it, and in many ways it probably did.

Bodie was watching the cowering creature in the corner and Ray stood looking at Diane and her two children. "That thing there," he said as he pointed to the creature in the corner of the front room, "I think is what is left over from the family that used to live here about two years ago." He took some cord from under the sink and went into the front room, then he tied the pathetic thing up tightly so that it could not move and kicked it into the corner.

Diane came in to him with an angry but confused look on her face. "What the fuck are you on about, Ray?" she shouted at him.

He spun on his heels and shouted back at her in a rage of anger, to he was using to mask his fear. "Oh come on, don't tell me that you didn't know. It was on the news and in the papers. Why the hell do you think we got the place so fucking cheap?"

"No, I didn't know and I still don't fucking know what the hell you are on about, Ray. What is happening? We must call the police!"

Ray reached into his pocket and threw her his mobile. She caught it and opened it, noticing that there was no signal, and she shook her head while she looked at him. "There is no signal, is there?" he asked calmly.

"No, there isn't. We have got to get out of here and report this to the police."

"Listen, Diane, you cannot go out there. Trust me."

"Trust you? I will never trust you again."

"About two years ago a police helicopter stumbled onto the atrocities that went on in this place. I will save you the details, but it was bad. Dead bodies in the lake, mutilated bodies in the house, dead dogs in the woods. It was not nice, and now I think it has come back to kick our teeth in." He looked at her and saw the horror in her face.

"And you knew all this and still brought us here? Do you think I would have come here if I fucking knew? You sick bastard, I will never forgive you for this, I hate you for this. We are getting out of here now, come on kids," she gathered her children and stood in the hall way.

Just then it happened, a thudding on the back door. A violent thudding and banging. Tommy screamed in blind terror, Amber was in shock and just clung onto her mother.

Ray checked the back door, seeing that it was holding solid. He called Bodie and went up to Diane. "Listen, you can hate me later, but right now we have got to pull together and get out of this mess. Whatever is out there wants to get in here." The banging got louder and harder, then the window was knocked in but the shutters held solid. The front door was knocked and hit again and again. Whatever it was, it was all around the house.

"What's happening?" Tommy shouted. "Make them go away, Mummy," he clung to her like he would never let go for the rest of his life.

"Upstairs now, everyone!" Ray ordered and they all ran up the stairs, Diane pushing her kids up first then following them, Bodie next and Ray taking the rear. He hustled them into the back room, then he went and got a chair from the front room and used this to reach up into the loft, through the trap door in the ceiling.

He pulled out his crossbow and arrows, bringing them into the back room, then crossed to the window, where he armed the crossbow, placing an arrow in the firing groove. He opened the window and leaned out, when he looked down he saw three figures at the back door. He knew there were more at the front. They were soaking wet figures of men, moving slowly and menacingly. They had come from the lake, victims of the family over the years. Somehow they had come back, come back to claim their revenge.

Ray aimed the bow straight at the head of the one nearest the door; he took aim through the sights, and squeezed the trigger. The arrow went, unseen by the human eye, from the bow and hit its target, the head of the figure at the door.

It dropped down awkwardly to the floor, the arrow stuck into the ground, the figure stuck momentarily with it, pinned and helpless. It just moved from side to side trying to break loose from the wooden shaft fixing it to the earth.

As Ray watched, he swallowed, realising what he was dealing with when the figure violently ripped its head from side to side, tearing large chunks of its skull with it, working itself free of the arrow. Looking up, the hideous face scowled at him with evil intensity and lifeless black eyes. The sight sent a bolt of fear through his body.

Tommy was crying and sobbing, Amber had wet herself and Diane was doing her best to calm them. "Oh, for fuck sake, shut him up, will you." Ray shouted at Diane.

"He is bloody petrified," she shouted back at him.

"Well it's not fucking helping matters."

"He doesn't understand, does he?" Diane was on the edge of a breakdown and her voice was faltering under the strain and the fear that gripped her.

"Oh, and I am suppose to know what the hell is going on, am I? I am just as in the fucking dark as everyone else here." Diane bowed her head and wept with her children, holding them close and hugging them in a protective way.

It was at that moment Ray realised and saw it, he was not part of that family. The family unit had cast him out, he felt alienated, an outsider and unwanted. He knew it might be his fault, but if he could get them out, then he was going to, and if it meant being alienated now and hereafter, then so be it. He had bigger things to deal with now, more urgent things.

He went back to the window, reloading his crossbow and taking aim again He singled out the same one and went for the rest of the head, the bit what was still hanging from the shoulders, the other bit was on the floor pinned by the first arrow. His aim was good and he hit it again, violently knocking it to the floor with the sheer force of the arrow.

Again it was temporary pinned to the earth, but again it shook itself free. Only this time it was unsteady on its feet, only about a quarter of the head was now on the shoulders and it was not functioning right. This gave Ray a surge of adrenaline, he reloaded once again; if he could slow it down with two arrows he might be able to stop it with three.

The pounding on the doors and shutters was getting louder and more violent. Bodie was growling and wanted to go down, but Ray forbade him doing so. He was staying next to his master and would do as he was commanded by the alpha male of the pack.

Ray's next arrow missed the target completely, his aim was off. Suddenly there was a smashing from downstairs, one of the shutters had given under the pressure. Ray put down the bow and ran downstairs followed by Bodie, going into the back room where the noise had come from. He saw a horrible, smelly, wet figure climbing through the broken shutter.

Bodie went up and jumped to his hind legs, ripping into the arm of the figure, tearing deep and strong, shaking his head so much power that the arm was torn from its socket, coming right off. Bodie dropped down to his four paws again, dropping the arm from his mouth.

At this point, Ray ran forward and, with all his strength, rammed into the shutter, knocking the figure back out and onto the ground under the window. He could see that the hinge had given way and he frantically looked around for something to wedge it back into position. He pushed and hit the shutter knocking it back to where it came from.

A thumping from the other side started to throw him back. Bodie was barking at the shutter, or rather, what was on the other side of it. Ray was stuck. If he let go, the shutter would give again and they would be in. If he did not get something to wedge it shut, he would be there all night. He looked desperately around, but nothing was within his grasp.

He looked up when he heard her voice. It was Diane, she had come down and was standing in the doorway. She looked tearful, frightened and confused, but functional, which is what Ray needed. Without another thought, he said to her urgently, "Under the stairs, get me the tool box, quickly."

"Yes," she said and went out of the room, only to come back moments later with Ray's tool box. She opened it and took out the hammer, Ray took it from her and started to hit the hinge back into its original position, bending it shut. He pointed to a screwdriver in the tool box. Diane handed it to him without question. He wedged this between the hinge and shutter, securing it again by hitting it home with the hammer.

He backed up and looked at her, she was scared and shaking. He reached out his arms and she rushed into them, sobbing into his chest. "I'm so sorry, babe. I am so sorry," Ray said to her, pulling her close and holding her tightly.

Bodie went to the front room and looked at the creature from the barn cowering in the corner. All of the banging now stopped for a moment, making Ray look up questioningly. Then, suddenly, it began again, but it was all concentrated on the front room, the same room the creature was in. The thing was terrified, curled up and whimpering and making inhuman sounds to itself.

Ray walked to the room, glancing at the shutters that he saw were holding. It did not hit him straight away and he didn't realise in the confusion. He called Bodie and left the room, going back upstairs.

Diane took Amber in her arms and rocked her gently as they sat on the bed, Tommy was sobbing next to his mother and Bodie stood guard at the top of the stairs. Ray looked down at Amber and saw she was acting strangely. She had fallen asleep but her breathing was a little erratic, and she looked pale. "What is up with her?" he asked.

"It's shock, Ray, fucking shock. I'm surprised we are all not suffering from it." Diane rested her daughter down on the bed and told Tommy to lay with her, which he did; they were both huddled together on the bed. Diane stood up and looked at Ray, she just did not know what to think, and she did not know what to do.

Rays face changed, something had come to him, and he looked at Diane. "They're not after us." he said calmly.

"Who then, Ray? What the hell is out there?"

"They're after the ones who put them in the lake. They want that little fucker down stairs." He ran down and Diane followed. The pounding was more intense and harder on the shutters, Ray went in and picked up the little pathetic body in the front room.

"Ray, what are you going to do?" Diane demanded.

"I'm going to give them what they want," he said, taking the skinny and shaking excuse for a living thing to the other front room. Diane followed, still not sure that she agreed with him.

"Ray, you can't just do that. It is a living being, a boy," she said looking at the creature.

"This thing just tried to kill your daughter and you are bothered about the little fucker?"

"Ray, stop, please. We have got to get help."

"We will get out of here, don't worry."

"Ray, please. What if it doesn't work? What if they are not after it?"

"Well, we have nothing to lose, do we? Now open those shutters when I tell you to." He picked the body of the small creature up, it weighed nothing at all, but it started to fight and try and break free of its restraints, and the pounding had stopped on the front shutters and back door. Ray knew he was right, they were coming to this window now; they seemed to know where the thing was. He got a good hold of the struggling thing in his arms, then he nodded to Diane.

She went to the shutters and unlatched them, quietly and slowly. Looking at Ray, she waited. He swung round like a hammer thrower and let the thing go out of his hands on the swing while Diane quickly opened the shutters and screamed at the hideous face staring in at her from outside. The creature that Ray had let go of flew through the air, crashing into the window glass and then going straight through it.

"Shut the fuckers," Ray shouted to Diane, who did just that, quickly, and locked them tight. They all ran upstairs and looked out of the bedroom window to the yard in front. They watched the small creature break free of its ties and stand there shaking. It was surrounded by seven figures from the lake. They towered over it and it was obvious that there was no escape for it.

What happened next made Diane feel sick. She had to put her hand to her mouth and look away, she could not watch the thing being pulled apart and ripped open. Each one of the figures from the lake grabbed a part of the small creature and started to rip at it, pulling and tearing at it. An arm torn off, then an ear, then the legs, all violently being ripped apart. Ray watched without speaking. The screams were terrible and would stay with anyone who heard them forever. You could never forget anything like that.

It didn't take long for the thing to be killed, ripped to pieces, lying in a pool of blood and body parts with its insides scattered over the ground. The figures now stood still looking at the blood-soaked ground. They seemed aimless now, swaying on the spot, not moving or shifting from their position. Ray watched this and didn't know what to make of it, what it meant. He looked back into Diane, who was looking at him from the bed.

"Is it gone?" she asked, tears in her eyes and wearing the saddest look Ray had ever seen. He felt for her more now than he had at any other moment.

"Yes, it is gone," was all he could say. He watched as she took his mobile from her pocket and tried to ring out again, but there was still no signal. She put it back into her pocket saying, "Why is there no signal? There usually is here." She looked up at him, tears welling up in her eyes.

"I don't know, babe, I don't know."

"I told you we should have gotten a telephone put in," she said. Unable to hold her tears back anymore, she cried and sobbed. Ray came over and sat next to her, putting his arm around her and giving her a hug. She leaned into him and sobbed on his shoulder as he rubbed her back. It ripped him apart to see her so upset and so scared.

"Listen, love, they all seem to be at the front. I am going to run out the back and go and get help. You will be safe here, I will leave Bodie and he will look after you."

"Be careful. I don't want to be left alone, Ray." She was muddled and not thinking straight, her words came out in the wrong order. He held her tight and tried to reassure her.

When he stood and went to the back room to look out of the window, his hopes of escape by that route were dashed. The water from the lake had come up to the house. He had no idea how it happened, but the murky water was all the way up to the bottom of the garden.

Floating atop the water were bodies, bobbing and moving on the water's surface. He did not know how many, he did not look long enough to count them. The water seemed to just stop at the garden's edge. He looked out across the lake, or where the lake should have been and saw a vast space. How could the whole lake just move like that?

CHAPTER 17

The howling started a short time afterwards. Diane was curled up on the bed with her children. She had taken Amber to the bathroom and got her cleaned up, then they all laid down together. Ray was watching the figures at the front and Bodie had his ears pricked up listening, he could hear them coming before anyone else could.

The howls got louder. Ray was looking at his car, regretting that it wasn't closer to the house. He put his hand into his pocket and took out his keys looked at them and then put them back into his pocket for no particular reason.

The figures then seemed to come back to life, they stopped just mulching round the pulp of a blood and guts on the floor and turned to face what was coming up the road.

"Diane, come here," Ray said, still looking out of the window.

"What is it?" she asked with a startled jump.

"Something is happening." She came to him and looked out of the window. "If I can get to the car, we might be able to fight our way out of here."

"We need to set fire to the barns, that way people will come, won't they? People will come, Ray, won't they?" her shrill voice made her panic apparent. He put his arm around her and kissed her on top of the head.

"Yes, people will come. We will get out of this and you will be safe, I promise."

Bodie growled and his hair rose on his back, just behind his neck. Ray looked at him with dismay. He knew something was wrong, knew that something was going to happen. He told Diane to go and sit back down. But she was looking out of the window, shaking and holding onto his arm. Her fingers were digging in and her nails marking his flesh.

It started with just one, then another appeared, panting and snarling, their eyes black like the figures from the lake, dead but staring, empty but menacing. There teeth were bared, and nasty growls and barks came from them. Many more came up from the road, from the woods; all different sizes, all in different states of decay, but all just as vicious and mad as the next.

It was soon apparent that there were at least fifteen dogs descending on the house. They all came into the yard, slowly stalking the figures that were watching them while unearthly snarls and yaps came from both sides. It was like some sort of macabre stand off, the living dead facing the living dead. Circling, the dogs got into position. It may have looked random, but they were very precise in their actions. The large bull dog was closest, then the large Alsatians, followed by big mongrels.

"What the fuck is going on?" Diane asked, shaking and breathing heavily through her nose.

"Fuck knows," Ray said as they both just watched. Then, by some sort of secret signal that all the dogs knew, and without warning, they simultaneously attacked.

The riot that followed was bloody and nasty, horrific. The dogs ripped at the lake figures, attacking without mercy and without conscience. All they wanted to do was kill and destroy. The fight was noisy and terrible, parts were being ripped off the figures, the dogs were being kicked and punched and ripped apart, the fight was like nothing ever seen by anyone on earth before. The carnage and ghastliness of the tearing of flesh and ripping of bone was something no man should have ever seen.

But Ray and Diane watched with a growing fear in their eyes and a terrible trembling in their stomachs. Even Bodie had come to the window, standing on his hind legs with his paws on the window sill. He was watching and growling wildly.

The figures that were down and being ripped apart were also being eaten by the smaller dogs. It seemed like a well-planned operation; the larger dogs took on the full frontal attack and the smaller dogs finished off the wounded and ate the dead.

Diane put her hand to her mouth, tears rolling down her face. She was not breathing right, it was too erratic. Her body was going into uncontrollable convulsions and she was losing control. Ray pulled her close and told her to stop looking. She turned and sunk her head into his shoulder, removing herself from the torture, from the gladiatorial spectacle in the front of their house, their home.

The dogs had no mercy, no remorse, they ripped and tore and lacerated their victims, soon all that was left was a pack of dogs eating at the remains of their kill. The few dogs that were destroyed were also eaten and discarded like the lake figures. The whole massacre had not lasted ten minutes. Now the figures were gone, nothing left but a mash of bones and bodies on the ground.

The dogs stopped and all looked up to the house, their eyes as black as the devil's eyes. They moved into a semi-circle and sat in front of the house, just watching, staring motionlessly.

Ray went back to the room where he had left his crossbow. He loaded it and, opening the window, he took aim at the biggest dog sitting in the centre.

"Where the fuck did you get that from?" Diane asked him.

He did not answer, instead aiming through the sight. The close-up shot of the dog's face showed just how evil it looked; dead, decaying, but so much menace and intimidation. And sheer evil. He squeezed the trigger and let the arrow fly. It hit the target perfectly, too perfectly; the power of the crossbow put the arrow straight through the dog. It jerked backwards slightly, but then just sat back and remained motionless, still looking at the house. The arrow going through it had no effect on it.

"Fuck!" was all Ray that said, dejected, disappointed and becoming tormented.

Then one large mongrel dog walked to the front door, it smelt the door step and went around the whole house, sniffing its way around. Ray saw it disappear around the side, then reappear on the opposite side a few moments later, it went to the large bull dog and sat down.

The dogs all lay down and just stared at the house. Confused, Ray looked at Diane, she looked at him just as confusedly.

"What does it mean?" she asked, watching out the window at the motionless dogs.

"I don't know, but it will be dark soon. We have got to get to the car."

"You can't, Ray, they will rip you apart!"

"Listen go and make us some food and bring us some drink, we need it."

"I can't eat," she said loudly.

"It will occupy your mind and we have to eat. We don't know how long this is going to go on for. They can't stay there forever, can they?" Ray insisted.

"Why not, why can't they stay there forever?" Diane bluntly asked.

"Make us some sandwiches and some drink, babe, please. And take Bodie with you."

"Ray, no one is hungry. We want to be getting out of here, not eating fucking sandwiches."

"I'm hungry and you must eat what you can. Please," he pleaded with her.

She turned and went to her children, asking them if they wanted a drink and some food. They both said yes, so she went downstairs, cautiously followed by Bodie when Ray commanded him to do so.

She looked around tentatively as she went. The house seemed empty, haunted, not like home anymore. Turning on the lights because the shutters had blocked out the daylight, she went into the kitchen and opened the fridge. Taking some meat out, she proceded to make some sandwiches for them all, guarded over by the loyal Bodie as she did so. Putting these on plates that she put on a tray with some milk, she returned upstairs to the front room.

Amazingly, they all sat in silence, eating, drinking and finishing their meal in a civilised manner. Ray took the plates back downstairs and fed Bodie and gave him water.

Meanwhile, darkness was fast approaching. Nothing else had happened, yet. The dogs just sat motionlessly staring at the house, waiting and watching. But for what only they knew. The night sky dropped in quickly, the place turned colder and a damp feeling came into the air. The house had become cold, moist, humid, and condensation formed on the windows.

Ray opened the window to let some air in, they were all in one room and their breath was causing the window to mist up, he thought. He went to the toilet and returned a little time later. He looked at the window and saw it was still wet, he thought the night air would have shifted it by now, so he wiped it with his hand, taking the wetness off and leaving a dry patch on the glass.

Turning to Diane, he asked, "Are you okay?" His voice was quiet and concerned.

"Why Ray? Why did you do this? Why did you con me and make me think you wanted to live with me here, me and my kids?" She was looking at him with distress in her eyes.

"I did not know anything like this would happen, did I? I was just curious about the place and its history, I never meant any harm to come to any of you." He came over and sat next to her on the bed. He put his arm around her, but she did not respond this time. She remained rigid.

"But you knew what this place was, what had happened here, and you lied to me. You still brought us here, and now we are all going to die and for what?"

"You are not going to die, we are going to get out of here."

"Why do you think that? No one ever comes here, no one ever did, why would they now? What the fuck are you going to do, Ray, just wait for them to go away?" She looked at him with a hint of hatred in her eyes. She pulled away from him and stood up, walking to the window.

Ray looked up and watched her go, then he noticed the window. He did not say anything, but he noticed that the spot where he had cleaned the wet off the glass was now damp again. It was as if he had never wiped it. It could not have misted back up that quickly.

Diane did not see, she just looked out of the open window at the waiting dogs. She shivered and folded her arms across her chest, saying, "You have ruined my life and the life of my kids. We put everything we had into this place and into you, and now we have nothing." her voice was sad and full of reproach.

"Diane, I am sorry," was all he could think to say, inadequate as it was.

"Not good enough. I loved you with all that I had, never have I given myself so totally to anyone before, and this is how you pay me back? This is how you treat us?"

Ray came up to her, he put his arms around her and tried to hold her tight in a warm hug but she twisted away and moved from him, then turned and faced him, looking him in the eye. "I fucking hate you for this," she said venomously.

"Well there isn't a lot I can say, is there? I love you Diane…"

She interrupted him before he could finish what he was saying. "Oh fuck off, you don't lie to and treat people you love like this, who are you trying to kid?" She shook her head and looked away from him, she was hurt and mad and frightened all at the same time and it was not easy for her to handle.

"I promise you, I will get you safely away from this fucking place." He was pleading with her to listen to him, something he had never done with any woman before.

"Your promises don't mean shit love, sorry. You have lied to me and I can never trust you again. You think more of that dog than you ever did of us," she nodded to Bodie, who was laid on the floor watching the scene in silence.

"Now that is rubbish, and you know it!"

"Do I? Do I Ray? You were never really comfortable with my kids, you were always having a go at Tommy, always saying nasty things," her voice began to break; she was hurting and didn't want to weaken, but was afraid she would not be able to stop herself.

Ray did not answer, he could see it was upsetting for her and he didn't want to make it worse. But by saying nothing he did. The silence was uncomfortable and the atmosphere made them both feel painfully unhappy.

She stared at him and, when he didn't answer, she just dropped her shoulders and cried. It was too much for her and she could not take it any more, she left the room and brushed past him, saying nothing more.

He watched her go and then looked down at the children, both asleep on the bed, huddled together for comfort and warmth. He did not know how to handle Diane's mood, he just did not know what to do. He had never chased after a woman in his life, they had always done that to him. But Diane was different, stronger and more independent, but she needed help and support now more then ever, and he just didn't know how to approach her.

He felt saddened and left the room, slowly walking down the stairs and into the living room. The place was still and silent. He walked to the kitchen and that is where he first noticed it. Water on the floor, cold and murky, and it was coming from under the back door.

He went to the door and put his hand on it. Why he didn't really know, but it was cold as ice. It must be the lake water coming nearer the house, and it was now entering the building. If the dogs somehow knew this, then this is what they were waiting for.

His shoes were wet and his feet felt instantly cold, this water was unnaturally chilly, he remembered when he touched it with his fingers. He had no idea how long they had, or how far the water would rise, there was certainly enough to engulf the house if the whole lake was to come up.

He put his head into his hands and shook his head. He had to make a move and quickly, it was no good just sitting here and waiting. He knew had to get help, or get everyone into his car and drive away, but how was he going to do it, he thought to himself.

He looked round and desperately wanted to see or find something that would help, but he didn't know what he was looking for and found nothing.

The water was seeping in past the kitchen now and out into the hall as he looked around in desperation. He dashed to the cupboard under the stairs, grabbing his large boots, then he ran back upstairs. He went to his wardrobe and started to put on several jumpers and his thick leather jacket, he pulled some more jeans on, then put the boots he got from under the stairs on.

Diane came to him and looked, then asked curiously, "What the fuck are you doing?"

"I'm going to get the car and bring it to the door. You try and cover me from the window with the crossbow. When I get the car near, you will have to dash to it as fast as you can. We're getting out of this fucking place," he looked at her without expression.

"You can't, those dogs will rip you apart," she said as she came closer to him, worried.

"Listen, we can not stay here any longer. The lake is coming in through the back door and we will be flooded out in no time. I must go for the car or we will drown, and seeing that I cannot swim anyway, I am going for the fucking car." He was determined and she knew she could not change his mind.

She picked up the crossbow and looked at him, he came over and showed her how to load it, with just actions, no words. Then he went down the stairs and into the kitchen, he took the largest knife he could find out of the drawer and then looked around for another weapon.

The best he could find was the handle of the mop, not much of a weapon, he thought but the best to do at hand. He stood on the mop head and snapped it off from the handle. He quickly evaluated his make shift armour, boots, jumpers, jeans and a jacket, he hoped it would give him a little protection from the bite of the dogs.

Diane came halfway down the stairs and looked at him, holding thecross bow in her hand, she wanted to go and hug him, but could not, she just said, "Be careful." It was totally inadequate, but it was all that came from her mouth.

"As soon as I am in the car, I will reverse it to the door, you let Bodie out and then you and the kids dash into the back." He took his keys and went to the front door, he took a deep breath and quietly turned the key in the lock to open it.

Diane dashed upstairs to the window, she leaned out and took aim at the nearest dog, then waited. She was shaking, nervous, but knew she had to pull herself together.

Ray was thinking of where the car was. He was hoping to get to it before any of the dogs got to him, the hardest bit would be stopping to unlock and open the door. He gripped the knife and the pole of wood he had, took a several more deep breaths, they got faster and faster, he was getting himself ready.

Then, without warning, he went, fast and hard. Opening the door quickly, he leapt out into the yard, he focused on the car as he closed the door behind him and ran.

Diane saw him go and as soon as the nearest large dog moved, she squeezed the trigger. Her aim was good and she caught it full in the chest, spinning it back and over. She did not look, she just reloaded the weapon.

Ray was dashing at top speed to the car, but the dogs were racing towards him as well, he knew he would not make it. He screamed out and lashed at the dog nearest to him, with the knife, he cut it full in the face and reeled it back. He kicked another hard on the jaw; he saw the jaw go limp and drop, broken. The dog's main weapon was gone, the dog was now relatively harmless, but these were no ordinary dogs.

Diane aimed and fired again, but her aim was off and the arrow missed everything and just ricocheted off the ground up and away, she reloaded once more as quickly as she could. By now, Ray was at the car, he had ran into it with a thud, and he kicked out and swung his knife and pole wildly, trying to hit anything in his way. The dogs surrounded him, they stood snarling and growling, he was breathing heavy, they seemed to be waiting for him to make a move.

He slowly took the keys from his pocket, he tried to reach back to door and put the key into the lock, almost there, he thought, just a little more. He was working blindly, keeping his eyes on menacing stare of his attackers. He fiddled a little, reaching down and behind him for the key hole, he was holding the knife and the keys in the same hand and it was making it more awkward. But he did it, the key went in. He glanced, just for a moment, down to the lock behind him. This was his mistake, the dogs attacked as soon as his stare was away from them.

They jumped and pounced towards him, he lashed out and hit one with the pole as he came around, but there were too many for him to be that lucky. One had his arm, he had tried to protect himself with layers of clothing but the teeth still hit his flesh. The pain was bad, but his adrenaline kept it at bay for the time being. He struggled and swung the dog on his arm around with him, he used it as a club and hit another pouncing, snarling attacker square in the mouth.

The pain in his arm was immense now, but he kicked out at a smaller dog, sending it reeling away. He stuck his knife in another and twisted it, but a second dog had gotten his leg, digging deep its vicious teeth. Ray screamed out in pain as the blood started to pour out of the wound. He frantically kicked and punched and fought the animals off, but it was becoming a losing battle. There were too many of them and they were too strong. He knew he had to do something and fast, or it would be over for him.

He gathered all his strength for one final push. He fought as if his life depended on it and, in fact, it did. Diane was in tears at the window, she could not fire the crossbow now even if she wanted to, the dogs were all too close to Ray. She was in a bad state, she saw the battle he was fighting and saw that he was losing, the dogs were getting the better of him. She looked around and saw the children standing behind her, terrified.

She gathered them up in her arms and told them to go to their room and kissed them both, then she went downstairs, calling Bodie as she did. He was only too happy to follow, he knew his master needed him.

Diane went to the door and opened it, she looked out and saw Ray struggling and fighting like a mad man. Bodie did not need any encouragement, he dashed over and instantly got hold of the dog on Ray's arm, he powered it down to the ground and went for its throat. He ripped and tore with speed and aggression, the dog did not know what had hit it. And it was lying in a mess of blood and flesh, ripped open and shaken senseless just moments later.

Bodie pounced onto the second dog, the large one holding his master's leg. Again Bodie went for the throat, but this dog was bigger and put up a fierce fight. They both rolled off, ripping and snapping at each other and the sounds they made were scaring Diane. She had not seen anything like it before.

Ray had gotten a brief respite, just what he needed; he managed to open the door as two of the dogs went to help their colleague with Bodie. He dropped into the car as pain ripped through his body. Slamming the door shut behind him, he put the key into the ignition and turned the engine over, he knew it would start first time and it did.

He sat up, shouting through the pain tearing at his limbs, then put the car in gear and went forward, straight for the dog looking at him from the front of the car. He ran it over and spun the car around fast, dirt drifting up from the tyres. He saw Bodie struggling with three dogs around him, snapping and biting at him. Ray put his foot down on the accelerator and hit the third dog, spinning it off to one side and shattering its back bone. He then turned once more and drove to the front door followed by two large dogs. He fell from the car and Diane helped him up.

"Where are the fucking kids," he shouted, not believing she had not got them ready

yet. They could have been away.

"Get in," she shouted and pushed him through the front door.

"Bodie, Bodie" he shouted, as he fell onto the floor inside the doorway.

His dog was getting up, exhausted and hurt, but still fighting. He managed to break

free and run fast for the house. Diane watched as the large animal pounded towards her,

followed by a pack of mad, unearthly dogs. Bodie ran past her and she slammed the door

shut, locking it as she did, screaming with fear as several of the dogs outside smashed into it.

She locked it, and looked around, Bodie had ran so fast that he had skidded on the wet

floor and ended up across the hallway. He was just now picking himself up and was limping

over to Ray, who was rolling on the floor in agony. Diane came to him and tried to help him

up but he rolled over, holding his arm, and she could see blood coming from his jeans and

jumpers.

She went into the kitchen where the water was about an inch high now all over the

ground floor. She searched in a high cupboard and found what she was looking for. Bringing

the first aid box back, she went over to Ray and helped him to his feet, then they all struggled

up the stairs and back into the bedroom. She put her shoulders under Ray's arm and took

some of his weight, she could see he was hurt and bleeding and needed help, she just hoped

she had enough supplies and energy to see to him.

Crashing onto the bed, Ray moaned out with pain. Diane took his jacket off and

pulled at his jumpers, she eventually got to the wound he was holding on his arm. It was a

nasty gash and she instantly knew that it needed stitching. She took some cotton wool and

disinfectant from the first aid box and went to work the best she could.

"Why were you not fucking ready? We could have been away." he shouted at her.

"You are in no fit state. Shut up." She pushed him back from the challenging posture that he had taken, she knew it had been a mistake not to have her children ready, but it could not be helped now, she had to get him patched up. She did the best she could and cleaned his wounds, bandaging them tightly as he laid down getting his composure back.

He looked at Bodie and saw he was licking at his own wounds, but was okay. He looked back at Diane as she was packing the first aid kit away. "Thank you" he said without looking at her.

"It was a stupid plan, you could have gotten yourself killed," she answered, not looking at him.

"We can get into the car now and leave. We have to be gone and soon." He started to lift himself off the bed, but she came over and pushed him back down.

"You fucking stay there until we are ready." She went into the other room and tried to explain to her petrified children what the plan was.

CHAPTER 18

The pounding at the door was louder, the dogs did not want to sit anymore, they wanted in. The ground floor was becoming flooded with the lake rising up to the house and time was running out, he knew it. Getting his breath back, he sat up. The initial shock was wearing off but he was still stiff and sore. He knew he had to pull it together or they would die. He looked down at Bodie and could see he was in pain too, it had been a fierce bloody battle for him and he needed to recover, but there was no time.

Ray stood and, a little unsteadily at first, went down the stairs. He walked through the ice-cold water, heading for the kitchen. Reaching under the sink, he took the claw hammer and crow bar that he stored under there. He had forgotten about these earlier, but it had come to him while he lay on the bed upstairs.

The water was coming in at a steady pace and soon would be flooding the whole place out. The hounds at the door were barking, growling and snapping at the wooden frame and door, trying to get in. It sent a shiver thought his spine to think he had to face them again. It made him grip the hammer and crow bar harder in his hand, his knuckles became white and the blood seeped from the bandages Diane had put on.

He could hear the crying from the kids upstairs and just knew this was not going to be easy from any angle, he took deep breaths and tried to calm and focus himself. The water was lashing over his boots and his feet were freezing. On ice cubes, he walked up the stairs and went to look out of the window. He could hear Diane shouting commands to her children about what they had to do.

He looked down and saw several of the dogs laid out on the floor ripped open and unable to move. Bodie had done a good job, it made him feel proud of his best friend. But there were still more, some sat waiting and looking at the house, one looked up straight at him and glared though deep black eyes, it sent Ray cold.

He gripped his two weapons and stared back, pulling his stare away only when he saw a dog smelling around the car. It sniffed, then scratched with its front paws around the tyres. A large mongrel of a dog, it then started to bite the tyres, becoming more and more determined, it bit and scratched at the rubber.

Ray looked over at Bodie, then walked to him and knelt down, putting the hammer and crow bar down. He took his dog in his arms and hugged him. Bodie responded by licking his face and hand. The bond was amazing, Ray knew his dog would give his life for him and the thought brought a lump in his throat. They embraced until Ray stood, taking the two weapons with him, and Bodie followed. They had both mentally prepared themselves and were ready.

"Diane, come on, we have to make a move," Ray shouted. He walked out of the room and saw Diane and her scared children with wet faces and tears rolling down their cheeks coming out of the other room.

They followed Ray down the stairs quietly. Water was gushing in through the back door, the whole downstairs was covered and it was reaching higher all the time. Ray looked back. "Me and Bodie will go out first and draw them away, you get into the car as fast as you can, do you understand?" he said with authority.

They all nodded, scared and shaking but they understood.

"Do exactly what I tell you, do you hear me?" Diane reinforced to her children.

"Right. The keys are in the ignition, all you need to do is start her up and you're away," Ray told her, he then looked away to Bodie before she said anything.

Both Ray and his dog went to the door, he looked back to Diane, he lifted his arm and threw her the crow bar. She caught it and got it ready in her hand, this was not just her survival, but that of her children too, and she was going to do all she could to get them away, safe and free.

Ray took a deep breath and opened the door. He dashed out, as did Bodie, but Bodie was met by two large dogs who pounced on him as soon as he left the door and powered and forced him back into the house. It was so unexpected and took everyone by surprise, Diane screamed and the children became hysterical.

Bodie was fighting for his life, ripping and tearing and savaging his attackers once again, but they were strong and Bodie was struggling. Being forced back, he was on his hind legs, snapping and baring his teeth. The water was gushing and making it difficult to fight. Further and further he was forced back into the house, past the stairs and past Diane and her screaming children.

Ray had brought the hammer down on a dog's head, smashing its skull into pieces, but it still came forward. He kicked it and broke its jaw, spinning on his heels he lashed out again with the hammer and caught another one full in the face sending it reeling off to one side. He lifted his boot and stomped on another dog near him. Knocking it down, he lifted his boot and broke its back legs by stomping on them. This dog barked and growled but could not get up. Ray continued to fight the wild animals, he was doing well and making good progress.

Diane opened the door, she could see this was her chance. "Come on now," she shouted to her children, and they all dashed from the house, scared and terrified but alive and wanting to stay that way. Only a matter of feet and she was there, hitting the car full on, she banged into it, hurting her arm but carried on. She opened the door and looked back, holding the crow bar high, she saw her kids running to her. But a dog was hunting Amber down and was almost on her.

Diane took aim and threw the bar in matter of a second, spinning it through the air, and hitting the dog full on in the face, it spun it off its feet, and the bar rolled away. Amber and Tommy were there and she pushed them into the car.

Looking up, she shouted to Ray, "We're in, come on, for fuck sake!" She shut the door as a dog jumped at it from the side, a second dog was chewing at the tyres and managed to burst one, and the car leaned down slightly to the left as the air seeped out from the gaping hole the dog had made. She started the car up and revved the engine, threw it into gear and took the handbrake off.

Bodie, at this point, was ripping at one his attackers, taking large amount of flesh with him as his powerful jaws tore, but he was bleeding and in pain, he was tired and getting bitten too many times. A third dog came in through the door and joined in the attack.

Bodie had three dogs to contend with now, he was on his hind legs and using all the strength he had, but three of them were too much and he was being pushed back more and more, as his strength was being drained more and more. The water was forcing the back door off its hinges and soon would be flooding the house completely. The cold was affecting Bodie, but it seemed to have no affect on his assailants.

Diane was screaming at Ray from inside of the car, she wanted him to get in. He was kicking at a dog, but dropped as a large, black bulldog pounced on his back and knocked him to the ground. It snapped at his head and throat, but Ray managed to restrain it by holding its neck with both hands, he pushed his thumbs in deep and tried to cut off its windpipe, but then realised it had no affect, the thing was already dead.

He twisted the head and forced it around and off him, a second dog rushed at him but he shrugged it off because it was not very large, and he managed to stay focused on the bulldog he had in his hands. He forced it violently down to the ground and shouted at it with anger and frustration. Its feet were scratching him and it was snarling, it was very strong and fighting with tremendous power.

Diane screamed as a dog jumped up onto the bonnet of the car and scratched at the windscreen, barking at her. The children curled up with each other and looked away, they were uncontrollable and in such fear that they could not think straight. They screamed and cried, holding each other on the back seat.

Ray finally managed to pin the black dog's head to the ground with his left hand, he lifted his right and smashed his fist down hard and fast time and time again on the side of the dog's bottom jaw, snapping it and breaking it. He stood, wary but in control, and again brought his boots down on the dog's back legs. They might be dead, but they can't walk with broken legs, he thought.

He looked around, there were still several dogs left, but they were small and circling him. He looked over to the car, exhausted and bleeding from his wounds, the old ones and some new ones. The dog on the bonnet was ripping the windscreen wipers off, Ray picked up the hammer and rushed over, he swung and hit the dog full on the side. Spinning it down onto the bonnet, he lifted the hammer and smashed the dog's head in. Time and time again, he hit it, leaving nothing but a pulp of blood and brains.

Pulling this dog off, he looked around just in time to catch an oncoming attacker square in the head as it pounced. Knocking to the ground, he kicked it and stomped on it like the rest.

"Get in, for fuck sake!" Diane screamed at him.

Looking up, Ray heard the yelp of pain of his dog Bodie, from within the house. "You get out of here," he told Diane, then headed back into the house. Water was rushing from the front door and out into the yard, he waded past the door and into the house where he saw three dogs attacking and getting the better of Bodie.

Shouting, Ray rushed forward through the water racing to help his dog. He reached him in matter of seconds. Grabbing the biggest dog, he lifted and spun it away, smashing it into the far wall. He kicked the second dog, the one that had Bodie pinned. He kicked it again and again until it let go and turned to face him.

Bodie struggled to get back to his feet even though the third dog was still at him and ripping into his neck, shaking its head. Bodie was hurt and went back down, the life being

dragged from him. The dog had hold and did not want to let go.

Diane did not know what to do, she moved the car away awkwardly with its burst tyre,

she heard her children screaming at her to move and leave. She looked back to the house.

The water was gushing out of the front door, the whole house soon would be engulfed and she

had to make a decision.

Ray brought the hammer down once again on a dog's head, again and again. It was

finally shattered and left to float away on the water. He turned and went to save his best

friend. He pulled at the dog that had its jaws around a weak Bodie's neck. It would not let

go, he pulled and tugged, but it growled and held fast.

Ray, in desperation, kicked and hit the dog with the hammer, smashing its back and

neck. He heard the bone crunch and break. The blows of the hammer destroyed the dog's

body, but not its killing instinct. Ray had to prise the jaws open and off of Bodie, he managed

it and just kept going, opening the mouth widely enough to snap the bottom jaw clean off the

dog. He pushed the body, still twitching, to one side. Bodie was underwater, he looked dead,

and desperately he lifted the large heavy dog free of the water and lifted his head.

The fear of losing him rose in Ray, he cried out, shaking the lifeless body of his dog,

trying to stop the blood coming from the wounds on the dog's body. His head spun around as

the third dog stood on the stairs looking at him, growling snarling and staring. Ray turned

and, with tremendous strength, lifted and put Bodie's body on the table. He then faced the

dog looking him. Water had burst the door open and the cold was unbearable, but Ray was in

a different state of mind at this moment.

He ran to the snarling dog in a fit of rage and madness. The dog pounced from the

stairs and they hit each other with full force. The dog snapped at Ray's face as he held it at

arm's length, smashing it against the walls and furniture. He was like a man possessed, he wanted this dog to suffer, this killer, this murderer.

Smashing the animal into everything and anything, he screamed at it, shouted at it and cursed it, the dog never stood a chance, it was smashed to pieces and broken beyond recognition. In a fit of madness, Ray destroyed the dog totally.

He was gasping for breath, his heart was pounding, but he froze momentarily when he heard it. A sound from behind him. He spun around and looked at the table. Bodie was trying to get up, he was alive. Ray ran to him with joy in his heart and relief in his bones.

He smiled at his dog and picked him up, struggling with the weight, but there was no way he was going to drop him now. He waded through the ice cold water, making for the front door and freedom. He reached it and ran out with the flow of the rushing lake cascading out of the house.

He struggled and walked in pain but with newfound strength. His mood was lifted even further when he saw his car reversing towards him. Diane had waited for him. He collapsed on to the back of the car as it reached him, his legs giving way under the tremendous weight of the soaking wet dog he had in his arms.

Diane got out and looked around, frightened but determined. She opened the hatch back and Ray threw Bodie in, crawling in after him. Diane slammed shut the boot and ran back into the car. She got into gear and drove out of the yard and through the gate, struggling with the burst tyre but getting away.

The lake had fully infiltrated the house, claiming it and smashing it to pieces. Rushing water filled the whole house, icy, dirty water that would destroy the whole place and sink it, dragging it into the lake, and taking with it the history, the fear and the horror of the old farm house. No one could return to the place, no one would ever inhabit the place again. The water washed away everything, from the bodies to the blood, the whole lot. And, finally, the house itself.

EPILOGUE

Ray was sitting alone in the dark barn. Totally alone. Diane and the children refused to set foot on the place again. It didn't matter that the house was gone, the dogs were safely disposed of, they would have none of it. Diane's ex arrived to spirit the children away to safety and, unfortunately, she went with them. "Just for the time being," she had said, "just until we can find another place to live."

He was tired of staring at the television at the hotel, tired of the thoughts that were warring in his head. He knew that he should have fought harder to prevent Diane leaving, he couldn't find it in him though. Her nightly phone calls only made him feel worse. And their call earlier this evening was the worst of all.

He knew he should just give the place up, let it go. They had spent all their money on the house, every bit that they'd saved. Diane was of a mind to find another place with the insurance proceeds, when they eventually received them. "Clever Diane, always thinking of everything," he thought ruefully, while thanking her for thinking of buying the insurance.

Unfortunately, that's where they disagreed. He wanted to stay on the property, build another house here. They could design everything, have it exactly the way that they wanted it to be. She would hear nothing of it. "I will not live on that land," she insisted. "I'm sorry, Ray, but you'll have to make a choice." It was a choice that he didn't want to have to make.

He thought of Bodie at the vet's office. It had only been a week since the incident, but he was improving even more quickly than the vet imagined he would. He missed his best friend, almost as much as he missed Diane.

He continued sitting in the dark, listening to the sounds of the night; the wind in the leaves, the twigs cracking under animal paws, the various chirps and calls of the woodland creatures.

Without being aware of what he was doing, he stood and walked slowly to the back of the barn, where the old machinery was still waiting to be discarded. His night vision was helped by the rays of moonlight cutting through the roof, beaming down as if to spotlight a pile of boxes that Ray hadn't noticed before.

It was as if he were watching himself from somewhere outside his body. He saw himself move to the boxes, taking the top box and putting it on the ground, doing the same with the next. When he reached the third box, the hair stood up on his neck.

It was the ouija board.

With trembling hands, Ray took the wooden board and planchette, moving to a clear area of the floor that was lit by another moonbeam, and sat down, placing the board before him.

He dropped the planchette onto the board and sat back, his heart pounding, a sweat breaking out on his forehead, watching as it began to move. Slowly at first, then faster and faster, spelling the same sentence every time. Ray thought his heart would explode as he watched, unable to move, unable to even breath. Reading the same message, again and again.

"It's not over"

The End............................   To be continued with Sisters of Darkness.....